Dance
with your
Heart

~ An SA Ballet Academy novel ~

BRONWYN MULROONEY

Dance with your Heart
By Bronwyn Mulrooney

Cover design and typesetting by RedRaven Designs
Cover photography by Lauge Sorensen

Print ISBN 978-0-620-71245-3

Web: www.saballetacademy.com
Email: info@saballetacademy.com

Follow SA Ballet Academy on Facebook, Instagram and Pinterest

Do you want cool, free stuff from SA Ballet Academy?
Become part of the SA Ballet Academy Fanclub!

To sign up, visit www.saballetacademy.com/fanclub/

For my ballet teacher, Mrs Symons,
who in teaching me about ballet, taught me about life.

Chapter 1

Gemma James sat on the wooden studio floor staring at her bleeding toes. The blisters from last term had barely healed and now there were a whole bunch more sprouting in their place.

She stretched out her legs and wiggled her toes. The stark white light from the fluorescent lights overhead bounced off the mirrored walls around her, leeching the colour from her feet and making them look even more ghastly.

At least her toenails had recovered. Hopefully they'd stick around this term and not go AWOL again.

"You're going to want to strap those up really well tomorrow," said a voice from over her shoulder.

Gemma caught Dineo peering down at the bloody mess that was her feet.

"I know. Don't worry, it'll be fine," she said, waving her friend away. The thing was, Dineo Nyathi had never had to worry about blistered toes and missing toenails. She may as well have danced out of the womb, *en pointe* no less. Everything about her was perfect – her lithe body, her lines and yes, her toes too.

"Aw! That's gonna hurt!" a chirpy voice in a fake

n TV accent piped up next to her.

_es already," Gemma said, pulling a face at her best friend Marley Moon Fields.

Like Dineo, Marley's dancing was near faultless, although she still got the occasional blister.

Gemma knew her friends meant well. It just niggled her that after three years at the South African Ballet Academy, she still felt like she wasn't good enough. Like she was the only one who still got blisters and had to strap up her feet.

A slender, petite dancer with flawless pale skin and huge hazel eyes, Gemma certainly looked the part. What she lacked in natural ability she made up for in her classes where she pushed herself hard, every day, to prove she deserved to be there. Gemma may not have been the best dancer, but she was definitely one of the hardest working students.

She turned away and stuffed her shoes into her bag. She'd deal with her toes back at the dorm.

Marley plonked herself down on the floor next to her and started undoing the ribbons of her *ponite* shoes. "So, first Friday night of the new term, you know what that means girls ..." she trailed off, a cheeky smile creeping across her freckled face.

"I don't know guys. Apparently The Banshee's doing patrols herself these days." Dineo's voice cracked with concern.

Gemma had heard the rumours. Some kids had been messing around after lights out and their detention-loving headmistress, Mrs Babington, aka The Banshee, had threatened to hunt them down herself and punish them.

Marley had coined the nickname because she said the strict head of the school screeched like a banshee and, according to her sources, in Irish mythology the banshee was an omen of death. The girls had decided being bust by The Banshee was akin to a death sentence, and so they'd christened the headmistress on the spot.

"But midnight feasts are tradition and you never break with tradition," Gemma said wagging her finger at Dineo. "Besides, I've found a great new spot for us, in a secret location, no one'll see us there. So 11pm tonight it is!"

Dineo sighed in surrender, prompting Marley to jump up and break out into her trademark victory dance, her wild strawberry blonde curls breaking free from her bun.

"That's why you're never going to land a lead role in this place. Like the rest of your little friends here, you dance like a spaz," a cool voice drawled from behind them.

Marley stopped her jig midstep and all three girls turned to see Aimee Atherton staring down at them. A sneer was plastered on her face, a hand on her hip. Her sinister sidekicks, Amber Goldstein and Naledi Mokoena, weren't far behind.

Gemma couldn't stand them – all from super-rich families and all of the opinion that everyone else had been put on earth to serve them. She was tired of constantly being harassed by the SABA Snobs or the SS, as she, Marley and Dineo called them.

Marley turned to face the gang leader. "Well at least it was our dancing that got us in here, and not our daddies' money."

"That's because your daddy doesn't have any money, darling," Aimee mocked, laughing.

Gemma stepped between the girls. "Oh shove off, Aimee. Go trim your broomstick or shine your cauldron or something," she snapped.

"Ugh … whatever," Aimee retorted, spinning on her heel to join the other two wicked stepsisters and disappearing in a puff of pink designer ballet gear.

That's why Gemma didn't like them. Not because they were rich, but because they rubbed it in everybody else's faces. Sure, she was there on a half scholarship and Marley's uncle paid for her schooling because her crazy hippie parents were too busy running a commune on his wine farm in the Cape, but still it irked her that they thought that made them better than everybody else.

Dineo's dad was a South African diplomat, based in China. Gemma had always wondered if that was why they left her alone.

The girls scooped up their stuff in silence and headed out of the cavernous studio into the warm spring sunshine.

Gemma loved the school at this time of the year. The jacarandas that lined the driveway formed an avenue of purple umbrellas and blanketed the lane and sprawling lawns in a fluffy carpet of lavender blossoms.

Forestlake Estate with its neatly trimmed English country gardens was alive and bursting with energy.

Even the grand old dame of a school building with its striking Herbert Baker design looked, like Sleeping Beauty, as though it had just woken afresh from its hundred-year slumber.

Gemma pulled the pins out of her bun and a cascade of raven hair tumbled down her back. She closed her eyes and throwing her head back, inhaled deeply.

"Hmmm …" she sighed.

"Uh … Gemma? Gemma James?" a voice she didn't recognise broke through her reverie.

Gemma cracked one eye open slightly to see a boy staring at her strangely.

"Oh," she gasped, embarrassed. She turned to face him.

Taller than her and a little closer to 14 than Gemma, he had dark hair that swept across his face. A pair of ice-blue eyes stared out from beneath his long fringe. He brushed it away and grinned sheepishly.

"I'm the new boy?"

"Oh right. I forgot about that." Gemma turned to Marley and Dineo. "New boy, meet Marley and Dineo. Marley and Dineo, meet new boy."

"It's Ethan, actually," he grinned again.

"Welcome to the madhouse," Marley said, thrusting her hand at Ethan.

Dineo nodded a polite hello.

"I'm showing Ethan around this afternoon," Gemma said.

"How'd you land that?" Marley asked.

"The Banshee spotted me just as Ethan was signing

in this morning. Do you guys want to …?"

"I've got to get back to the dorm," Dineo interrupted. "I need to get at least three hours in this afternoon. Don't forget to soak those toes tonight," she shouted over her shoulder as she took off.

"Sorry Gems, I promised to call my mom this afternoon," Marley said. "See you later?"

"Uh … okay." Gemma suddenly felt self-conscious, stranded with the newbie.

She looked at Ethan. He smiled, melting some of the awkwardness.

"They seem nice," he said, watching Dineo and Marley disappear down the stairs to the dorms.

"They are," Gemma agreed.

"What does Dineo do in the afternoons?" he asked. "Three hours of …?"

"Ballet," she said. "Dineo's a perfectionist. No, she's worse than a perfectionist. She's a deranged perfectionist on a suicide mission. She spends every spare second holed up in her room practising," she explained, knowing that Ethan was probably wondering why someone would possibly spend their spare time doing more of the very same thing they'd spent most of their day doing already.

"That's why she's the best junior dancer in the school," Gemma said.

"Figures … she looked kind of serious, you know?" he frowned playfully.

Gemma laughed, turning towards the gardens. "She is. The first time we met her, she actually shouted at us, like a teacher!"

"So did you all meet here, at the academy?" Ethan asked, falling in step alongside her.

"Yup. Well, actually I met Marley at the auditions. She was in my group, thank goodness."

"Was it hectic?"

"Totally! I was terrified! We were only ten and I was really nervous. But Marley's like little Ms Sunshine, nothing gets her down. So she helped me. Plus she spotted that I hadn't tucked in my ribbons just as we were going into the studio. So if it hadn't been for her …" Gemma dragged her finger across her throat, her head falling limply to one side and her tongue hanging out. "I'd have been out of here before I even got in."

She remembered the day she got the news that she'd made it. Her mom's cellphone rang, and she heard her talking in that funny posh way when it was somebody she didn't know on the other end. "Oh that's wonderful news!" she said as Gemma had quietly sidled up to her to try listen in. "Yes, yes, I understand, I'll tell her. Oh thank you so much!" she gushed and had barely hung up when she turned to Gemma and grabbed her. "You're in! You're in! Honey you made it!" she screamed, hugging Gemma.

It was a dream come true. It was the one thing Gemma wanted more than anything in the world. She'd been accepted to the SA Ballet Academy, the most prestigious ballet school in Africa and the only place to train if you were serious about becoming a dancer.

And serious Gemma was, although her insatiable sense of adventure combined with Marley's crazy sense of humour meant life was anything but dull at SABA.

Ethan laughed at Gemma's actions as they walked past the studios.

"Dineo was already here," Gemma continued. "She's been here since she was like two or something! We kind of ran her over in the corridor outside the theatre one day. By mistake!" Gemma stressed in response to his surprised look. "That's the day she shouted at us. Marley was impersonating Mrs Siyankovsky – she's the pre-junior ballet mistress ... Russian ... crazy old bat – anyway and we were laughing like mad and walked around the corner and kind of knocked Dineo right over! We didn't even see her. She was so angry with us. But then Marley broke out into her wild Russian ballet mistress routine again and we kind of lost it again. Even Dineo had to laugh. We've all been friends ever since. Marley and I share a dorm too, which totally rocks. What about you – how'd you land up here?"

"I was born in Joburg, but after my mom got a job with the English National Ballet we moved to London for a few years. But she's just retired so we moved back to South Africa."

"Wow!" Gemma stopped walking. "She was a principal?" Ethan nodded.

"So how long have you been dancing?" she asked.

"My whole life, really. Since I was two. A side-effect of having a dancer for a mom, I guess. I started here but have been at the Royal Academy of Ballet and Dance since we went to the UK."

"That must have been amazing!" Gemma enthused,

steering Ethan towards the sports fields.

She hoped he wouldn't turn out to be like Charles Crawford-Bradshaw or Percival Wetherby. They were the two guys who claimed the top spots alongside Aimee in the SS. They were both rich, rude and also had links to top London ballet schools.

"Well, this is our version of the Royal Academy," she said, turning and waving her hand in the direction of the school. From the hockey field where they were now standing, the school looked imposing and impressive.

The academy was really special for Gemma. She loved the fact that the building was a hundred years old. Like a dancer past the prime of her life, it was still beautiful, just a little aged on the outside.

Stone steps led up to a portico punctuated by white columns that framed two colossal arched wooden doors. The rough-hewn stone walls loomed large above the entrance, spreading out into the two separate wings that were now the girls' and guys' hostels.

Hundreds of Venetian windows lined the walls like huge eyes keeping watch over the estate. Gemma wondered what all those eyes might have seen over the past century, and what secrets were contained within those old walls.

Ethan was taking it all in too. "It's cool. Kinda creepy, but cool."

"I know, right? It's really old. It was built in 1916 by the famous Johannesburg randlord John Smythe, for his daughter who wanted to be a ballet dancer." Gemma was totally addicted to the history of the estate. "He …"

"What's a randlord?" Ethan interrupted.

"The randlords were like mining bosses in the old days. You know, they controlled all Joburg's gold mines and were super rich and powerful. They built these big estates. Can you just imagine this place back then? The dancers, the ballets they performed … and the guests – the ladies in their pouffy dresses and the men looking all dapper in their suits." She hitched her thumbs under two imaginary trouser braces, just like the men did in the old days, lifted up her chin and strode ahead of Ethan in an old-fashioned manly kind of way.

Ethan chuckled at Gemma.

They had come full circle and were now back where they'd first started.

"Well, there you go," Gemma said, "that's SABA."

"Cool! Thanks! Will I … uh … see you around?" Ethan asked.

"For sure!" Gemma smiled, before bouncing down the stairs and heading back to her dorm at Fonteyn House.

Gemma couldn't wait for the midnight feast. She knew the girls were going to die when she revealed their new secret rendezvous. Three very long hours after lights out she finally tiptoed over to Marley's bed.

She nudged the lump. Marley's eyes shot open and she sat bolt upright.

"You scared me!" she said, taking her earphones out of her ears. She was listening to meditation music on her phone. "Is it time?" she whispered.

"Yup, now haul your lazy butt out of bed."

The girls dressed by torchlight and grabbed their stash of chips and chocolate. Gemma opened the door a notch and listened. The dorm was quiet. She slipped out and gave the dimly lit passage the once over.

"All clear," she whispered.

The two tiptoed down the corridor and softly knocked on Dineo's door four rooms down.

Two minutes later all three were quietly padding through the dorm to the new hideout. The school was eerily quiet. Old-building creaks and groans echoed around them.

Gemma thought about the school's legends – that Forestlake Estate was haunted. Apparently old ballet mistresses wafted down the halls at night and some people even claimed to have heard dancing in the old abandoned studio.

And then there was the story of the Halloween Ghost.

Gemma vividly recalled her first Halloween at the school. It was well after lights out, the school was quiet. A loud screech followed by an almighty crash echoed through the school. The whole place woke up and eventually everybody was congregated in the entrance hall.

Even The Banshee was there, still dressed in her floral pyjamas and slippers, curlers in her hair. She'd called the security guard who'd followed the direction of the noise to Ms Dubois' studio. He had discovered Mr Rose's beloved Steinway baby grand piano flung across the room and shattered into what looked like a million toothpicks on the floor. That was when she'd first learnt of what the students had nicknamed the Halloween Ghost.

The school had blamed vandals, but then last year someone had ripped the wings from the stage, pulled down the lighting rig and trashed the green room. And nobody had heard a thing.

Gemma didn't know if she really believed in that stuff. She was curious about it, but real ghosts … she wasn't sure.

Still, the spooky stillness about the school tonight made her understand why others would fall for such stories. The place definitely had a supernatural air after dark.

She led the girls to the abandoned ballet studio at the back of the building. Nobody used the old studio. Gemma didn't know why. And no one ever went there. Especially not at night.

"Guyssss," Dineo hissed. "This is where The Banshee heard those kids this week. She's probably here."

"We'll see her coming – she'll need a torch," Gemma whispered, flicking on her own penlight to reveal a set of heavy double doors.

She tried the handle, and the old doors creaked open. Dust and the smell of aged rosin floated up, filling her nostrils. A shiver of excitement vibrated through her. She crept into the studio. Marley followed with Dineo cowering behind her.

"So what do you think?" she smiled proudly.

"Cooool! Nice going, Gems" Marley whispered, impressed.

Gemma closed the door and pushed the others into

the centre of the room, floorboards groaning beneath their feet. An eerie silence descended as they took in the antiquated ballet studio. It was bathed in silver light flooding in from the full moon that was perched just outside the enormous arched windows. Crystal chandeliers dripped dusty old cobwebs that hung from their arms like upside down fairy castles.

Gemma flashed her torch around the room. Soft glows leapt off the mirrored walls, the light and shadows alternating in a ghostly *pas de deux* across the wooden floor.

"This place is a dump, let's go," said Dineo flatly.

"Can't you imagine dancing here like a hundred years ago? Imagine their dresses and their shoes," Gemma said pirouetting across the floor to the barre on the far side of the room. Her reflection flitted ghost-like in the faded mirror.

Suddenly, the floorboards cracked beneath her.

Gemma lost her balance.

She stumbled.

She lurched for the barre.

The wall gave way.

And she was gone.

Chapter 2

It was pitch dark. And cold.

Gemma was on the floor with no idea of how she'd got there. She shivered.

Where was she? And what had happened to her torch? A pale white glow flickered in the corner of her eye. She turned to it … and her breath caught in her throat. The light wasn't coming from her torch, it was coming from something else.

In the corner.

Something that was watching her.

She gasped, clamping her hand over her mouth.

"Gems?" came a voice to her right. It was Marley. And she had her torch.

Gemma was too scared to answer.

"Gems!" came the more urgent call.

"I'm in here," Gemma squeaked.

The next minute Marley and Dineo were next to her. "Oh thank goodness! You know you unlocked some kind of a secret room when you grabbed the barre …" Marley stopped suddenly. The torch light was illuminating Gemma's horrified expression, her gaze still fixed on the glow in the corner.

Marley followed her eyes. "Oh …"

Dineo gasped.

Marley elbowed her friend in the ribs. "Sshhh … don't you dare scream."

She hauled Gemma up off the floor. "Are you okay?"

"I guess." Gemma's voice wobbled as she grabbed Marley's hand.

The three girls faced off with the one standing in the corner. The one very pale girl in a frilly nightgown with hair down to her waist. The one who was staring at them with huge dark eyes in a really strange way. The one who was very clearly … not human.

Gemma's heart hammered out a terrified staccato in her ears. She squeezed Marley's hand.

The girl cocked her head in Gemma's direction, black pools glaring at her.

"It's okay," Marley soothed, totally at ease. "This room, it's your place? We're sorry for disturbing you," she said softly.

The girl moved forward an inch, looking from Marley to Gemma. "Who are you? What do you seek here?" her sad hollow voice echoed around the room.

"Uh … I'm Gemma," she stammered. "This is Marley and that," she jerked her thumb backwards over her shoulder, "is Dineo. We're dancers, at the academy. I kind of fell through the wall over there, by accident …"

If ghosts could relax, she did. Something Marley and Gemma had said had taken the edge off. Slowly she moved closer to the girls. She stopped just metres in front of them.

"I am Emily. I am pleased to make your acquaintance."

"We really didn't mean to bother you. We didn't even know this place existed," Gemma said.

"No person does. You are the first people I have seen in a hundred years. I am Emily Smythe."

A hush fell over the room. It was as though everybody was holding their breath as they digested her statement.

Emily was John Smythe's daughter? Gemma had just been telling Ethan about John Smythe. But he'd had only one daughter, Gemma thought. Which meant he'd built the school for this girl? But hadn't he opened the school when she was 16, in 1916? Emily had just said she hadn't seen a soul in a hundred years. It was 2016 now. Did that mean she died the same year? At only 16?

Only when Gemma heard her own whisper did she realise she'd spoken her thoughts aloud.

"Yes, I was 16. I died here. In this very room. I … I … took my own life," Emily said sadly.

Her chilling declaration hung in the air.

Gemma was shocked. What awful thing could have happened to make her do that? And if it was so bad, why was she still here in the school?

"I know spirits sometimes get trapped in the places where they die. Has that happened to you? Is that why you're still here?" Marley asked gently, seemingly reading Gemma's mind.

Emily nodded.

"We could help you …" Gemma offered. "Do you want to tell us what happened?"

Marley smiled at Emily encouragingly.

"But we …" Dineo started to protest, but Emily was already nodding and sinking silently to the studio floor, her nightgown puffing up around her.

"I was an only child, raised by my father after my mother died. I had always wanted to be a ballet dancer. My father took me to the ballet when I was a child. We used to sit in the royal box and watch the dancers. I fell in love with the graceful swans and sylphs of the stage. But more and more, as his work took him across the country to other mines, so he had less and less time for me and my dreams.

I was lonely. I do not know if it was out of a genuine desire to see me happy again, or out of desperation to get me out the house, but my father declared he would build a ballet school, just for me. And he did – he got the best architects to design the most magnificent school and hired the most outstanding ballet masters and mistresses he could find, mostly from England, France and Italy.

I was sweet 16 and this was his Valentine's Day gift for me as he believed ballet was my only love.

It was my first love, of that he was correct, but it was not my only love. My father believed I had no admirers, but I did. I had befriended a young man named Oliver Black, who was the son of the school's new caretaker."

Emily's face seemed to brighten at the mention of Oliver.

"We had met two weeks before the school had opened when Oliver found me sobbing in the rose garden. My father had asked me to live at the academy when it opened, as he would be travelling a lot in the future. I was angry and confused, and ran away to Forestlake Estate. That was where Oliver found me. He was sweet and gentle and kind. He lifted my spirits and made me laugh, and so our friendship begun.

As the weeks passed we spent a lot of time together, unbeknown to my family. Once the school opened, I stole away every spare moment I had just to see him. I soon realised I had fallen in love with him. My first true love!" Emily whispered, looking up, lost in the sweet memory of her first love.

She looked at the girls again. "Oliver said he felt the same and wanted to marry me as soon as I was finished with school.

Then something awful happened. I woke one morning to stories that Oliver had left Forestlake Estate to get married. To someone else! I left the school immediately for home. Upon my return home, my dear cousin Clarence Cornwell confirmed the news. He said Oliver had in fact married that morning. He comforted me as I cried, for days on end."

Emily's face twisted with anguish, betrayal clouding her stark features.

"I was beside myself and lonelier than ever, so I returned to the school the next morning. All I wanted was to see Oliver again. But I knew that would not happen. A life without Oliver was no life at all, and so I took my own."

Early on the morning of 31 October 1916 Emily had hung herself from a beam in the only place she'd ever been happy – the ballet studio they were now in.

Gemma felt awful. She could feel the despair and heartache rolling off Emily. It seemed to engulf them in the small room. That, and anger.

She wondered if it was Emily's anger at Oliver that kept her here – more of an emotional barricade than a physical one.

"You … you said 31 October?" Dineo winced.

"What?" whispered Gemma, nudging Dineo in the side.

Emily regarded Dineo quietly. "Yes."

"Are you the Halloween Ghost?" Dineo blurted out.

Emily nodded.

The girls froze as the realisation sank in.

"I am sure you are wondering why I only make my presence known on Halloween and not the rest of the year? It is something I have pondered the past one hundred years. It is as though I am allowed out on that night that I took my life, but no other night. To look for Oliver, perhaps? To find the answers I seek? I am not certain. I can wander anywhere I want but at dawn's first light I find myself back in here. In this room. Trapped for another year."

"Is it maybe looking for those answers that keeps you here? Is that what you're waiting for? To know what happened all those years ago?" Gemma asked softly.

Emily shrugged. "Yes. I still want to know why. I can't let it go. I love him but I can never forgive him. Never. I am tired now, tired of this earthly prison. But I need to know what happened so I can find my peace. Finally."

"You must be very lonely. What do you do the rest of the time?" asked Marley.

Emily smiled gently. "I dance. My dancing is all I have left."

That would explain the dancing people had heard in the old studio at night. And maybe even the "kids" The Banshee had heard up here recently.

"So the noises up here, that's you too?" Gemma asked.

Emily almost looked sheepish. "I've been a little agitated lately."

Marley had been quietly figuring things out. "So you can't leave this room because it was closed up and cut off from the rest of the school after you killed yourself. For some reason you can escape on 31 October every year but that's all?"

"Yes, but your friend here opened it tonight, so now I can finally get out."

"Uh, get out where, exactly?" Dineo's voice trembled.

"Into the rest of the school. To visit the places I used to love. The ballroom where Oliver and I used to dance when the school was empty, the library where we used to meet, my old room …"

Dineo's eyes widened in alarm. "You mean haunt the school?"

"I've been biding my time here for a hundred years listening to symphonies through the wall and wishing that it was me still dancing, me on that stage and me living my dream. But it is not," Emily almost spat.

Gemma could see now why Emily had glared at them at first. She was bitter. She felt betrayed and jealous that the school that should have been hers now belonged to others. That she'd been left with nothing but a broken heart and the shadow of a dream she would never fulfil. But maybe she'd found a kindred spirit in them, as dancers, and maybe they could help her after all.

"We can find a way to solve this. Really we can," she said.

"Oh crap, but not tonight," Marley gasped. "It's past 2am already!"

The girls jumped up. "We'll be back, soon. And we're going to help you," Gemma promised as they made a beeline for the broken wall.

"Will you really?" Emily asked softly.

The girls stopped.

"Yes. Yes, we give you our word," said Gemma, turning to face Emily.

There was something different about the pale girl, Gemma thought. Then she realised: Emily now had a glimmer of hope.

"We'll come back for you," Gemma added, smiling.

She quickly followed Dineo and Marley through the opening in the wall.

"Oh," she poked her head back through the hole. "And try not to scare anybody until then, please?"

Back in the dormitory, Gemma climbed into bed but couldn't sleep. Slivers of moonlight were playing havoc with the shadows on the wall.

A noise above her made her sit up. How had she not recognised it before? That wasn't the sound of the old building resting its bones at night or kids messing around.

It was unmistakably the sound of feet softly skimming the floor. Of *bourrée*s and *chasses* and dainty *pirouettes* on demi-*pointe*. Emily was dancing again. Gemma fell asleep listening to her ghostly twirls around the room to a haunted melody her human ears couldn't hear.

Chapter 3

"And one, and two and, Gemma stop frowning, you not going to funeral, no? Aimee, Aimee your back, straighten, you look like bag of potatoes!" Ms Dubois trilled above Mr Rose's piano, her strong French accent masking her broken English.

She was putting the girls through their paces at the barre and being particularly demanding.

"Ah, some of you swinging today. Keep those hips square," she motioned with her hands in front of her, "and no swinging. You want to swing, go to the park! *Grand battement en croix* again please, Mr Rose. And one, and two, soft hands, Marley, you must hold baby chicks in your hands! Like that, you are crushing them!"

They'd been at it for two hours already and Gemma was exhausted. She'd battled to fall asleep last night and with their early call, only ended up getting three hours' sleep.

She forced herself to focus, concentrating on Ms Dubois' direction.

Three hours later, the thirty red-faced and "glowing" girls (according to Ms Dubois, girls didn't sweat, they glowed!) were sprawled at the petite teacher's feet.

"Now girls, this year the academy hosts a special centenary celebration. The school is one hundred years old, no? Yes, so we're putting on a special performance this year. The Grade 7s put on one full-length production and the Grade 12s, another ..."

"Does that mean solos?" Aimee interrupted. "Some of us are so ready for solos," she drawled. "Well, some of us more than others," she tossed over her shoulder in Gemma's direction.

"Some of us just deserve it more," Amber shrieked, as excited chatter rose around them.

"Yes, yes, exciting," Ms Dubois said loudly. "You want to know which ballet, yes? It will be the same as the first ballet performed here in 1916. You will perform *Giselle*."

Ms Dubois held up her hands. "Ssh ... ssh girls, girls! *Giselle*, hmmm, beautiful ballet. One of the best!" the ballet mistress gushed. "*Giselle* is the story of a peasant girl who dies suddenly. Her ghost comes back ..."

Gemma shot Marley an OMG look.

"... to protect her, how you say, her, her lover from evil spirits. There are only two leads, one boy and one girl. But also other solos. Yes? Good!"

Aimee notched her chin higher and turned to face her friends. "Well with me being Giselle that leaves two solos for you guys. How awesome is that?"

"You'll be the best Giselle ever, Aims," Naledi prattled.

"Now, we'll be casting in just three weeks' time. I want you all to shine, girls, shine!" Ms Dubois raised her hands up in the air as though she were praising the heavens. "So, hard work ahead, yes? The schedule is up, so please keep checking it. We will be doing *pas de deux* work with the boys as well in some classes ..."

Excited giggles erupted around the teacher.

"That means we'll see the new boy!" Gemma heard someone behind her say.

"Oooh yes!" giggled another.

"Well I'll be paired with Ethan, of course," Aimee stated matter of factly to no one in particular.

"... so you must check the schedule!" Ms Dubois was shouting now. "Okay, okay, off you go, shoo, shoo," she said, waving the gaggle of girls out the door. "See you all on Monday, girls!"

"Wow, leads! And solos!" Gemma beamed, turning to face her friends.

She'd been dying for a shot to show everybody just what she could do on that stage. And finally, here it was. A chance to prove that she belonged up there. Belonged in this school. That she was as good as the others.

And her best friend knew that. "It's totally rad," Marley nodded. "I'm sure you guys will get solos," she said, looking at Gemma encouragingly.

The excitement was infectious – even Dineo was smiling. "It's going to be great! Our own production, with our solos and *pas de deux*!"

Her rare display of emotion sent Marley and Gemma into a fit of giggles.

"What, I'm allowed to be excited, aren't I?" Dineo retorted, turning for the change rooms.

"Of course you are, you're just, funny, that's all!" Gemma laughed falling into step alongside her, linking her arm through her friend's.

The girls changed out of their gear, each quietly mulling over the morning's developments. Suddenly Gemma remembered Emily. "Gees, with all this stuff about the production I almost forgot about last night! What are we going to do about ..." she gave a furtive glance over her shoulder before leaning in and whispering the last word, "Emily?"

"You mean what are you going to do – I don't want anything to do with her. Besides, we've got *Giselle* to focus on now," Dineo said flatly.

"We said we were going to help her and I think we should," Gemma shrugged. "Unless you want her loose in the school? At night? In the dorms ..."

"Ugh," Dineo shivered.

Gemma grinned cheekily. "Thought not!"

"Relax Neo, we'll figure something out. Who knows, maybe dealing with a real live ghost will help you prepare for your role as Giselle? I mean, she becomes a ghost and all," Marley shrugged.

"You know how dumb that sounds, right? Real live ghost?" Gemma teased.

Marley rolled her eyes.

Gemma jumped up, pulling Dineo along with her. "Come on, let's go check the schedule and then it's time for a little ghost rescue planning."

Ms Dubois had posted the girls' gruelling schedule for the coming weeks on the noticeboard. Five hours of training every day, broken down into two hours of normal class and three hours of *Giselle* prep. Wednesdays' and Fridays' *Giselle* classes would be held with the Grade 7 boys to learn the *pas de deux*. The production itself would take place the first two weeks of December.

"Eek, that's hectic!" Gemma grimaced.

Marley just nodded, staring blankly at the intimidating timetable.

Dineo's eyebrows shot up. "Tight schedule. Have to be ready by the end of November. Hmmm …" She was working out how she was going to fit all the extra training into her already jam-packed day.

"Oh well, we have this weekend still to do some stuff before all that starts. So come on gals," Gemma wiggled in between Marley and Dineo and, throwing her arms around their necks, guided her friends towards the doors.

"That looks like a ghost right there." Gemma and Marley were lying on their backs on the grass in the sun, cloud watching. Gemma pointed to a white blob in the sky. "See, there's her arm, her head, a long white dress."

Marley giggled.

Dineo was looking up *Giselle* online on her phone and pretending to ignore them.

The gardens were quiet. All the seniors were out – they got weekend privileges – and the pre-juniors were at the Joburg Theatre watching a Joburg Ballet production.

"I think it's not knowing why Oliver left her and married someone else that keeps Emily trapped here," said Gemma, her mind wandering back over Emily's sad story. "I think if we could figure out why he did that, and tell her, maybe then she could rest in peace."

"Yes, that would work," Marley said, flipping onto her stomach.

Marley knew a lot about paranormal stuff from the two summer holidays she had spent helping her mom in a little esoteric shop in Cape Town where she had worked. Marley had always been interested in worlds beyond the physical, and had picked up what was now proving to be very useful information from listening to her mother talk to customers.

"Spirits hang around when they feel they have unfinished business," she explained. "So helping her understand that should help her to get to the light."

"Huh?"

"The light. You know, heaven, or wherever it is we go after we leave here. When people die suddenly they sometimes still think they're alive. For like, years and years afterwards. So they stay here and don't go to the light, because they don't know they have to. But knowing the truth helps them. It sets their spirit free."

"But how are we going to find out what happened?" Gemma asked.

"What happened to who?" Gemma recognised Mitchell Peterson's voice instantly. She sat up and saw the slender boy with the wild hair curiously peering down at them.

"Hey Mitch!" she smiled.

"Gemmmms," Mitchell boomed, bowing down low with his arm across his waist like some kind of mad page boy. "The ever lovely Marley," he bowed again, "And my dearest Dineo," a third bow.

Marley laughed. "Hello kind sir!"

Dineo barely raised her eyes from her phone, giving Mitchell a half-hearted wave.

"I believe you've already made the acquaintance of my dear friend here, Lord Blake?"

Ethan seemed to pop out of nowhere from behind Mitchell.

"Hi," he grinned at the girls.

"Hello, Ethan," Gemma said.

"Hey new boy!" chimed Marley.

"So what, lovely ladies, happened to whom, and why does this trouble you so, pray tell?" Mitchell said in his poshest accent.

Mitchell was an excellent actor. Like Marley, he was forever clowning around and putting on different accents or imitating people. He had 27 facial expressions in his repertoire and could perfectly imitate 38 different sounds, from an aeroplane taking off to a hadeda's cry.

Gemma and Marley exchanged looks. They both knew what the other was thinking – should they reveal their secret to the boys?

"Uh, just a little puzzle we're trying to figure out," Gemma said vaguely.

"Maybe we could help?" Ethan offered, striding over and dropping down on the grass next to her.

"Yes, come on, out with it," Mitchell demanded, grabbing Dineo's foot and shaking it for emphasis.

"Don't ask me, I know nothing about ghosts. Besides,

Gemma's the one who's so keen to help her ..." Dineo suddenly realised what she'd said. She looked up from her phone at Gemma and Marley. "Sorry," she mouthed silently to her friends.

Mitchell's face lit up. "Whoa, ghosts? Tell me more, ladies, tell me more!"

Gemma looked over her shoulder furtively. "We kind of found the Halloween Ghost last night," she whispered.

"You kind of found it? What?" Mitchell drew back in shock.

"You can't tell anybody, okay?" Gemma said quickly.

"Okay, okay," he said.

"No swear on it, you really can't tell anybody else what we're about to tell you. Promise!" Gemma insisted, turning to Ethan and including him in her earnest plea.

The boys solemnly swore to secrecy, crossing their hearts.

Gemma and Marley told the boys what had happened the night before and their theories as to why Emily remained trapped in the old studio.

"If we don't do something, she's going to torment the school! She's already wrecked the theatre, who knows what'll be next?" Gemma stressed.

"So we need to find out what happened to Oliver and why he left Emily, then she should be cool, right?" Ethan asked looking at her.

"Uh, yes. Well, we think so," she said.

"So what do we do next? Can we see her?" asked Mitchell, jumping up.

She regarded the boys sceptically. "No, you can't. And what's this 'we' business, hmmm?" she asked, tilting her head to one side cheekily.

"We can help you guys. It'll be like a covert SABA operation," Mitchell said, holding an invisible walkie talkie to his mouth. "Sierra Alpha Bravo Alpha 1 come in, come in," he said in a crackly two-way radio voice complete with static.

Marley giggled. "Yes! You can start by helping us think of where to find the information we need to piece this story together."

"Any teachers who might know something?" Ethan asked.

Gemma laughed. "There's a lot of old fossils knocking around this place, but none a hundred years plus!"

Ethan burst out laughing. "I meant, someone who might know the original story, who maybe who knew the Smythe family?" he clarified.

"Not sure really?" Gemma said, looking over her shoulder at the old school as if the answer might magically appear out of thin air.

"What about the school library?" Ethan offered. "It's got an archive section – Ms Shaw showed me yesterday. Maybe there's something in there?"

Chapter 4

"Now, what did you sweeties say you were looking for again?" Ms Shaw asked, looking up from the filing cabinet, her glasses perched on the tip of her pointy little nose.

"Information on the Smythe family?" Gemma gently reminded the old librarian.

"Oh yes. It's in the school archives, love. But a little disorganised if I do say so myself. Try looking in the school history and family history sections. Oh, and the section on Mr Smythe, there's lots of information there too," she said, waving them in the general direction of the archives.

Gemma turned to Ethan. "This was a good idea."

"Thanks!" he smiled.

Although the files were all over the place, they'd been thoughtfully compiled, Gemma noticed, looking at the meticulously marked and dated files in the family history section.

Suddenly one caught her eye. It looked different. No name, no date. Just simply E.R.S on the spine. Gemma slowly pulled out the file and opened it.

It was about Emily!

There was a birth notice, early brownish pictures of Emily with what must have been her mother, and Emily as a young girl with her father. There was Emily in her first ballet outfit. Emily on the stage at a concert. And Emily dancing around the garden in her satin slippers. She looked so happy, Gemma thought. The last picture was of Emily standing on the stone steps at the entrance to the school.

That was it. Nothing more.

Taped to the back cover of the file was an envelope.

Gemma pried the envelope free and opened it. Inside were three pieces of paper. The first was the marriage notice of Oliver Black. The second was a newspaper clipping with a photo taken at Oliver's wedding. And the third was his death notice. She studied each one. Something niggled her about the photo from the newspaper. Then she spotted it.

"What?!" She gasped.

Gemma's mind was racing. It couldn't be, she thought.

"What's wrong?" Marley whispered. She and Dineo were suddenly standing next to her.

Gemma was shaking her head. "You're never going to believe this."

Mitchell and Ethan appeared from behind a bookcase.

"There's a photo. In this file on Emily. A photo from Oliver's wedding. It was in the newspaper. Look here," Gemma held up the clipping for them to see. She read the caption. "This is Oliver's parents," she pointed to a couple next to the groom. "And this is the bride's parents. But this," she pointed to a man peering out from behind

Oliver's father, "is Clarence Cornwall. Remember, Emily's cousin. The one who told her that Oliver had married someone else!"

Marley registered first. "Oh wow."

"What was he doing at the wedding?" Mitchell asked, confused.

"Exactly. What was he doing there?" Gemma said suspiciously.

"Maybe he went there to try persuade Oliver not to marry this, what's her name …" Ethan leaned over to get a better look, "this Lily girl?"

Marley shook her head. "He wouldn't be in the wedding photo."

Gemma bit her lip as she thought. "He looks creepy. He almost looks like he's leering at Oliver, who doesn't even look happy. Look at his face," she stabbed Clarence's face with her finger.

"What does the article say?" asked Ethan.

"I'm still reading it, but nothing much yet. Just when the wedding took place, stuff about the two families … apparently the bride and groom's sides were both very poor. Wait, it says the wedding was a surprise. And was made possible by a mysterious, wealthy benefactor. Who treated the entire community to a banquet to celebrate … it must be Clarence!" Gemma exclaimed. "He's the only wealthy person in the picture. But why would he pay for the wedding when he knew how much Emily loved Oliver, and he her? It makes no sense!"

"He wanted Oliver out of the way?" Ethan offered.

The pieces started to fall into place for Gemma. "He

was in love with Emily! Clarence, he wanted to marry her! And Oliver was just some poor school caretaker's son. So he offered the two families money, forcing Oliver and Lily to marry. That would clear the way for him to comfort Emily, gain her trust and make her love him instead! I bet you that's it. Oliver never left Emily for Lily. He was paid off by her own cousin!" she said incredulously.

"But why did he do it. Oliver, I mean, why didn't he refuse?" asked Marley.

"Blackmail," said Mitchell.

Everyone stared at him blankly.

"Blackmail. Like in the movies you've got something I want. I've got a hold over you. So I blackmail you to get what I want. Easy!"

Gemma tried to follow his train of thought. "So Oliver had Emily. But Oliver and his dad were employed here by John Smythe, who was Clarence's uncle. So Clarence threatens Oliver, saying if he doesn't agree to marry Lily, he'll do something and he and his father will lose their jobs. They're poor. They need to work. If they lose this job, they'll probably never work in this town again and will have to leave. But Oliver needs to stay here, to be with Emily. So he agrees. For his sake and his father's. And marries Lily."

"But he still loves Emily so much, that when he finds out she's dead, he kills himself too," Marley finished, holding up the death notice that Gemma had forgotten all about.

"What?" Dineo spoke up for the first time.

"Yes! And get this, on the same day as Emily!" Gemma gushed. "Look – 31 October 1916! It's like he just couldn't live without her."

Dineo was dumbstruck. "Oh my word."

"Blah blah blah … 'died by his own hand'… blah blah… It doesn't say how he died though?" Mitchell said, reading the death notice from over Marley's shoulder.

"Nope," Gemma said, shaking her head. "Only that he killed himself, just like Emily did."

"Wow. That's so Romeo and Juliet …" Ethan mumbled.

Gemma arched one eyebrow. That's a surprise, she thought, a boy knowing the intricacies of a Shakespeare love story. Romeo and Juliet was her favourite Shakespeare play.

Ethan caught Gemma's surprised look. He thumped his heart with his right hand, tilting his head up towards Gemma. "But, soft! What light through yonder window breaks?" He threw his hand up towards the library window. "It is the east," and faced Gemma again, reaching up to her as he threw himself dramatically over the table between them, "and Juliet is the sun."

Gemma clapped her hand over her mouth as she stifled a loud belly laugh.

"Well said, young chap," Mitch said, slapping Ethan's shoulder.

Gemma was still laughing. Ethan was quoting Romeo from the famous balcony scene, but he had the most ridiculous look on his face as he lay stretched over the table towards her.

Marley joined in and soon they were all clutching

42

their stomachs, laughing at Ethan.

"Shhh!" someone shouted from across the library.

Gemma was struck by Ethan's subtle confidence. He was nothing like Charles and Percy. He was confident but not arrogant, and he could laugh at himself too.

Ethan shrugged. "Sorry, dad was an English professor so I kind of know that stuff. Back to Emily and Oliver," he whispered, sitting upright in his chair again. "So we have a possible story, but I think we need proof. I mean we're just guessing here? How do we know if we're right?" Ethan asked.

Everyone was silent.

"We could ask Emily?" Gemma whispered hopefully. "We have to tell her anyway, that Clarence was there that day. And that Oliver didn't run off and live happily ever after with Lily after Emily died. We could ask Emily if Clarence had ever said anything about her relationship with Oliver, or if he'd hinted that he actually wanted to marry her?"

Dineo was sceptical. "How's she going to remember that? It was a hundred years ago!"

"Spirits retain all the knowledge of their lives on earth. Time means nothing in that realm," Marley confirmed. "That could work. Seriously, she's the only one that would really know."

Ethan's face lit up. "Cool, so let's go tell her!"

Gemma thought for a second. "Hmm, we'd have to go tonight."

Dineo was already shaking her head. "No way. Uh uh. You can count me out."

"What, you not up for a little ghostbusting, girlfriend?"

Mitchell mocked.

"No, I'm not, actually," Dineo retorted, standing. "I've got stuff to do. I'll see you guys later, okay?" she told Gemma and Marley before turning for the library door.

"This is not really her thing," Gemma said quickly. "But you guys are up for it?" She was kind of grateful to have the extra back-up, given the complete weirdness of the situation.

"For sure!" Ethan beamed.

"Great!" said Gemma. "But there are some ground rules you have to follow if you don't want to get bust by The Banshee. Or hack off our ghost. So listen up."

"Gemma?"

Gemma could clearly pick out Mitchell's shadow from the darkness that was shot through with silver from the still-full moon outside.

She flashed her torch on and off. Suddenly the two boys were beside them.

"This place is cool at night!" Mitchell breathed excitedly.

"It gets better!" Marley whispered in anticipation.

Gemma led the group across the landing to the old studio. She gingerly turned the door knob and the double doors gave way. Her heart raced.

The group had agreed earlier that it was best that she and Marley go in first and tell Emily that Ethan and Mitchell had joined the great ghost rescue mission, but now that they were there, she was a little worried about how the already testy spirit might react.

She grabbed Marley's hand and the two girls disappeared into the moon-dappled studio.

It didn't take long to spot Emily. She was sitting on the window ledge in the corner, knees hugged tightly to her chest, staring out at the night.

"Emily?" Gemma whispered.

Emily turned to face them, her face seeming to light up. "Gemma, Marley, I have been awaiting your return!"

"We have some news for you," Gemma said enthusiastically.

Emily hopped down from the ledge. "Oh please do tell me," she said, floating across the room towards them.

"First we wanted to introduce you to two new friends who are helping us. Would that be alright?"

Emily regarded them quietly, as though she was considering Gemma's offer.

She shrugged. "Yes, that would be fine."

"They're here now. Can Marley go get them, so you can meet them?"

Emily nodded.

"They're very good friends of ours," Gemma said after Marley had left. "They want to help …"

Gemma broke off. Emily's eyes had widened perceptibly. She'd just spotted the boys.

Mitchell and Ethan were trailing behind Marley, eyes as big as saucers fixed on Emily.

Gemma could tell from where she stood they could barely believe what they were seeing.

Emily sized up the newcomers.

Gemma sensed the boys were going to have to earn Emily's trust. "This is Mitchell and this is Ethan," she gestured. "They're also dancers at the academy."

"They are … boys," Emily said coolly.

Marley suddenly caught her drift. "Oh yes, but they're good guys. I promise, they're here to help us, not to hurt anyone."

Gemma realised Mitchell and Ethan weren't only going to have to earn Emily's trust because they were new, but because they were boys. Emily's last encounter with a guy hadn't gone down too well.

Ethan broke the silence. "It's very nice to meet you, Emily," he said sincerely.

Emily looked from one to the other.

"Uh, hi," Mitchell smiled, clearly at a loss for words for the first time in his life.

Emily seemed to defrost a little, but turned her back to the boys to face Gemma. "You said you had news for me?"

"Yes! Good news, we think," Gemma smiled. "We found a file in the Smythe family archives in the library that had a photograph in it, taken at Oliver's wedding."

Emily grimaced.

"There was a person in the photo," she continued. "We're not sure why he was there, or that he even should have been there at all. It was Clarence. Clarence Cornwall."

Emily looked shocked. Gemma could see she was trying desperately to understand.

"There was an article next to the photo. It said that

Oliver's family was very poor and that a wealthy benefactor had paid for the wedding. We were wondering, could Clarence have been the benefactor?"

"That does not make any sense," Emily whispered, shaking her head.

"We also discovered that Oliver ... well ... he died too. The same day as you. He also killed himself ... on 31 October 1916. We believe he never wanted to leave you after all. He never wanted to marry someone else. He still loved you! And when he found out what you had done, he killed himself as well."

Emily stared at Gemma in disbelief. "He still loved me?" her voice quivered.

"That's what we believe," Marley said gently. "We think maybe Clarence paid off Oliver to marry someone else so he – Clarence – could marry you instead."

It was as though Emily had been punched in the stomach; her ghostly aura flickered for a second as she processed the news of Oliver's death. One silvery tear slowly slid down her cheek.

The room fell deathly quiet.

"He still loved me," Emily repeated, this time in a whisper.

Gemma waited, then softly asked, "Did Clarence ever tell you that he wanted to marry you?"

There was a long silence as Emily pondered the question. She slowly nodded her head.

Gemma could tell Emily had just realised something.

"Yes," she said finally. "In a way, I suppose. He had always said I would make a lovely bride and a beautiful wife. He was always bringing me presents and he would stay with me when father was away. We saw him sometimes, Oliver and I, when we were in the gardens. I think now, I think now he might have been watching us. Oh no! That would explain why he never liked Oliver. He was always terribly mean to him. He must have seen us, and been jealous. I … I never thought … oh!" Emily choked on her words.

"Was Clarence the kind of guy who'd actually blackmail somebody?" Marley probed.

Emily nodded slowly again, her voice just a whisper. "Yes."

"You also said Clarence confirmed the news of the wedding to you, that morning. We think he wanted to be the first to tell you so that he could comfort you and gain your trust so that you would marry him," Gemma added.

Emily started sobbing. "Oh yes, you must be correct. That is exactly how he was that day … and the next morning when I left. It must be so," she wailed. "Oliver died because of Clarence, because of me!"

"Oh no, you can't feel responsible. You didn't know what was going on," Marley soothed.

"But I do feel responsible. This is all my fault. Oh how will I ever right this wrong?" Emily cried.

The group was silent. They didn't have the answer to that difficult question.

"Maybe if we knew what happened to Oliver, we could fix this situation for both of you?" Gemma offered.

"Do you know where Oliver died? Perhaps like me

he is still here somewhere, at Forestlake Estate?" Emily suddenly asked.

Marley shrugged. "We don't know, but we could try to find out."

"And that might help us with our plan to get you out of here," Gemma added.

Emily smiled sweetly, as though a great weight had been lifted from her. "I would be most grateful."

Mitchell and Ethan hadn't said much, but pledged their allegiance to the cause when Gemma and Marley again promised to find a way to free Emily from the school.

Ethan and Mitchell offered to walk the girls back to their dorm. Silently the four made their way through the deathly quiet Fonteyn House. The boys bid Gemma and Marley goodnight before disappearing into the darkness.

Gemma closed the door behind her. She knew tonight an important piece of the puzzle had fallen into place. And she knew Emily would be more desperate now than ever to get out.

But what she didn't know was that someone had been lurking in the shadows just beyond the passage.

And that that person had just seen them return from their late-night rendezvous, with two boys in tow.

Chapter 5

"Gemma! Marley!" Dineo's impatient calling was coupled with a bout of banging on the dorm door.

"I'm coming," Gemma yawned, stumbling out of bed and unlocking the door.

"Gees, are you guys deaf? What are you doing in here?" She burst into the messy dorm room. The girls' clothes from last night's outing were strewn across the floor, the curtains were still closed and there was little sign of life.

"Sorry, had another late night last night," Gemma yawned again.

"Obviously. Did you forget we're meant to be working on our natural sciences assignment today?" Dineo asked tersely.

"Um … no, what time is it?" Gemma asked.

"It's 8:30," Dineo answered, picking up the open ballet bag that was on Gemma's desk, and dropping it onto the floor before sliding into the chair.

"No, we haven't forgotten, but it's sooo early!"

"Arghhhh …" Marley groaned, rolling over in her bed.

It was far too early to do science assignments, Gemma

decided, so she surreptitiously began telling Dineo what had happened the night before.

She told her about introducing the boys to Emily, Emily's reaction to the story and the revelations about Clarence.

"So we were right," Marley's sleepy voice declared from behind Dineo.

"Great. Problem solved, now we can get on with more important things," Dineo said, nodding approvingly as she opened her science file.

"Mmmm, not yet. We still don't know what to do with Emily. How do we get her out of the school?" Gemma asked.

"Why do you have to do anything with her at all? She knows the truth now, isn't that enough?" asked Dineo.

"We promised we'd help her rest in peace. Think of it this way, if we don't, she could turn into an angry ghost that's trapped here, with full run of the school. That's even worse. Like, she could be here right now, standing right there behind you and you wouldn't even know," Gemma added, pulling her nightgown over her head and doing her best Emily impression behind an unsuspecting Dineo.

Marley giggled and Dineo, guessing what was going on, tossed a book over her left shoulder, hitting Gemma on the head.

"Aw!" Gemma yelped.

"Well, when you put it like that, I suppose," Dineo continued. "I'm focusing on *Giselle* now, so I won't be joining you on your excursions. Just tell me when she's gone."

"Well, we have the boys to help us now," Gemma said. "So you're off the hook."

"Speaking of which, I think our new boy has a little crush on you, Gems," Marley said cheekily.

"What? No he doesn't," Gemma said, feeling her cheeks colour. "Why on earth would you say that?"

"I've seen him watching you. A lot. Not in a creepy way, in a nice way."

"Argh, that doesn't mean anything. I really like Ethan, but just as a friend. He's funny. And he likes Shakespeare too. And he's a nice guy."

"A pretty gorgeous nice guy …" Marley fluttered her eyelashes.

Gemma laughed at Marley. She wasn't really into guys. None of them were. Sure, they noticed cute guys and there were a couple of good-looking seniors in the school that the junior girls had crushes on. But while some other girls their age were all about boys, boys, boys, they were all about ballet, ballet, ballet.

"Well, as nice as he is, Ethan's not going to do our science assignment for us," Dineo said, tapping Gemma's pink 'I love ballet' ruler on her still open natural sciences file. "So, how about we do this thing then?"

"Okay, but breakfast first. Please?" Marley made a sad puppy dog face at the same time that Gemma's tummy let out a huge growl, prompting all three girls to burst out laughing.

The cafeteria was abuzz with talk of the *Giselle* training that started the next day. Around mouthfuls of cooked oats, cornflakes, muesli, yoghurt and fruit, girls discussed who would be best suited to which roles, with almost every conversation being punctuated with the words "solos", "*pas de deux*" and "the boys".

Gemma suddenly realised the magnitude of what was about to happen to her and her fellow students; the opportunities presented to them through this ballet and the way they used them could make or break their dance careers.

Gemma's phone beeped. It was a message from Mitchell.

When can we meet to chat about Mission Emily?

After lunch? Working on astronomy assignment this morning

Cool. Summerhouse at 2?

Cool

"That was Mitch," Gemma said, tucking into her hot oats. "They want to meet at two at the summerhouse to discuss you know what."

The morning went by quickly as the girls worked furiously to finish their assignment. By lunchtime they were done and grabbed a quick snack before heading off to meet the boys.

Mitchell and Ethan were already at the summerhouse, a pretty open-air gazebo where bands used to play in the old days. It was resplendent with its white Victorian lace iron detail and a steeply pitched roof with a tall spire on top that made it look like it had fallen right out of a fairy tale. A tumble of wild roses and jasmine that spilled down the side of the roof and along the back like a delicate curtain added to its charm.

Mitchell was bouncing in his seat like an eager Jack Russell. "So, got any ideas for our rescue mission then?" he asked once they'd all found a seat – Marley and Gemma on one side of the gazebo opposite the boys, and Dineo tucked away on the far side, her nose in a book on advanced ballet techniques.

"Nope," Gemma raised her eyebrows. "You guys?"

The boys shook their heads.

"How do you rescue a ghost anyway?" Mitchell asked looking at Marley, who had become the resident ghost guru.

"Welllll …" she drew out the word as she collected her thoughts. "There are many ways to do that. First you have to help the spirit resolve whatever issue is keeping them here. Remember how we said spirits get stuck on the earthly plane when they have unfinished business? Emily's unfinished business was not knowing why Oliver had abandoned her when they were supposed to get married …"

"Which she now knows …" Mitchell interrupted.

"Yes, but the new information of Oliver's suicide has made her feel responsible for his death – that's more unfinished business for Emily," Marley said. "So to release her we really need to …"

"Find Oliver!" Gemma blurted.

Three faces stared blankly back at her.

"Well, somehow she needs to not feel responsible for his death anymore. Assuming he's also trapped at the school, maybe finding him will somehow help her forgive herself? Then she can release that memory and go?" Gemma offered.

Marley nodded. "That could work."

"But how do we know if he's here?" Ethan asked.

Mitchell scratched his head. "And how do we find him if he is?"

The group was quiet, lost in thought.

"Anything else strange that happens around the school not connected to the Halloween Ghost?" Ethan asked.

"Not that I know of," Gemma shrugged, diverting her gaze away from the group to the grounds beyond.

'What do you know about Oliver?' she silently asked the old school.

She was suddenly aware of a group of people headed their way: the full SS complement – Amber, Naledi and Aimee flanked by her two notorious henchmen, Charles and Percival.

"Hi Gemma, Marley ..." Aimee said as the pack reached the summerhouse, looking from one girl to the next, her high-pitched voice dripping with fake sweetness. "Dineo," she said a little more flatly, looking vaguely at the far corner. "We saw you sitting here and thought we must come say hello," she said, dusting a non-existent piece of lint from the shirt that was falling perfectly off one shoulder.

"Hi," Amber and Naledi chimed in unison from either side of Aimee.

Gemma and Marley nodded silently. Dineo didn't

move an inch, strategically concealed behind her book.

What was Aimee up to, Gemma wondered, thinking how her saccharine sweetness was clearly a cover for some ulterior motive.

"Hi Mitchell," Aimee purred at the gobsmacked Mitch. She'd never said a word to him in his entire time at SABA. "And who do we have here?" she asked, turning to face Ethan.

"Hi, I'm Aimee," she said, pulling her long blonde ponytail over her tanned shoulder. "And you are …?"

Suddenly Gemma was all too aware of Aimee's intent – she'd set her sights on Ethan, and was being super nice for his benefit.

"Ethan," he said standing up to greet her. "Hi!"

"Nice to meet you, Ethan," Aimee batted her eyelashes, "I heard you've transferred here from the Royal Academy in London, is that true?"

"Yes, we recently moved back to South Africa, so here I am," he said, looking from Aimee to Amber and Naledi who were all coy smiles for the new boy.

"Charles," Charles said, stepping forward from behind Aimee where he and Percival had been deeply engaged in conversation, and shaking Ethan's hand.

"And Percival," Percival added, doing the same.

"I was just saying to Percy here that I heard your mother was a principal dancer in the old Johannesburg City Ballet Company years ago," Charles said.

"Yes, she was. That was before we moved to London," Ethan said.

"My mother was also a principal in the company, I

wonder if they knew each other?" Charles asked.

"I'm not sure, I'll ask her," Ethan said cheerily, completely unaware of the giggle of girls to Charles' left who were summing up Ethan from top to toe.

"Hello Gemma." Charles turned his attention to Gemma. Tall and blonde, he was like the guy version of Aimee. His posh accent, gleaned from European au pairs who'd tutored him before he joined SABA, sounded more like it belonged to a debonair old man than a thirteen-year-old boy. Well, he was a snob, so it figured, Gemma thought.

"Hello Charles," she replied curtly, not sure why he always made a point of greeting her when he was so mean.

Last year he and Percy had spiked old Mr Rose's egg mayonnaise sarmies with fresh chillies, causing him to abandon his piano mid-concerto and make a mad dash for the staff canteen where he downed two glasses of water so quickly, he had hiccups for the rest of the afternoon.

And that was after they let five disgustingly ugly Parktown prawns loose in the cafeteria one dinner time.

Boys and girls started screaming; the more the enormous crickets jumped, the more the students jumped too, out of their chairs, onto each other and even over the counters into the kitchen!

Amidst the pandemonium, one prawn landed on Cook Sheila's apron sending her shrieking for the garden and deserting her pots at the stove, which all boiled over.

Poor Timmy Thomas in Grade 3 had such a fear of

jumping insects, in his haste to get away he ran smack bang into a pillar and knocked himself out cold.

Probably worst off was Sam Brookes in Grade 5. A prawn was perched right on the top of her head. In all her screaming and shouting for help, her sister Michelle lunged for the cretin with a giant soup ladle, missing the prawn completely but connecting Sam square in the left eye. She broke her nose and had a black eye for weeks.

Charles and Percy had been behind their fair share of school pranks, but also much of Aimee's dirty work.

She just had to click her fingers and they were there, ready and waiting because, Gemma was sure, they'd both had the biggest crush on the blonde heiress for the longest time.

Unsuspecting learners' shoes had landed up in trees, their *pointe* shoes stripped of their ribbons, and leotard straps cut off, all thanks to Charles and Percy. And all at Aimee's instruction, because those girls got on the wrong side of her.

Aimee was now standing in front of Ethan. "I see you've already made some … friends." She winced at the last word. "If you want to have any kind of decent rep in this place, you're welcome to join us." She looked disdainfully in Gemma and Marley's direction. "You really don't have to hang out with the local riff raff."

"Uh, thanks … I think," Ethan said.

"Ok well, nice meeting you," she cooed over her shoulder as she turned to leave the summerhouse. "Toodleloo," she said, snapping her fingers for the rest of the SS to follow.

"I'm guessing they're not your favourite bunch of people?" Ethan said after they were out of ear shot.

"No. They're rude, rich and obnoxious. And they prey on everyone else who is not rude, rich and obnoxious," Gemma said.

Marley shook her head. "They're just royal pains in the you-know-what! We've got far more exciting things to think about now, like solving our Oliver mystery …"

"And preparing for *Giselle*." Dineo spoke for the first time, snapping her book shut and standing up. "It's almost curfew, so we need to get back to the dorms." She clutched her book to her chest, folding two petite arms around it, and turned to Gemma and Marley. "You guys coming?"

There was a 5pm curfew on a Sunday; all students, except for the Grade 11s and 12s, had to be back in their dorms by 5pm. This was followed by dinner at 6pm and lights out at 8pm.

Dineo was a sucker for school rules, and made sure her two friends stayed in line. Well, as much as possible anyway. Gemma always thought of her as a fussing mother duck, trying to keep her unruly ducklings in check.

Gemma stood up and hugged her friend. "Yes, we're coming!"

Marley joined in. "Dineo, sarmie!" she yelled.

Dineo gave her friends a wry smile. "Come on then," she said, ducking out of the tangle of arms that engulfed her and sashaying down the stairs of the summerhouse.

"We'll catch up with you guys tomorrow?" Gemma

said to the boys, as she and Marley turned to follow Dineo.

"Cool, bye!" Ethan said, looking directly at Gemma.

Mitchell was clutching his heart and staring vacantly at the girls, his left hand waving robotically.

Gemma laughed to herself; he was still recovering from Aimee having spoken to him for the first time ever. She had that effect on people, Gemma thought.

The noise in the studio was deafening. All the Grade 7 girls and boys were seated on the floor waiting for Ms Dubois, The Banshee and Mr Milano, the school's ballet master, to arrive.

Mr Milano was Italian, hailing from what he called "the ancient home of ballet – Italia!" He still had traces of his Italian accent, and when he got really excited, these were stronger than ever. He reminded Gemma of a passionate cook in a bustling kitchen, shouting orders and motioning wildly with his hands.

Whenever a new ballet was staged, all the SABA heavyweights attended the initial briefing, with Mr Milano addressing the dancers directly. He would then work with the class ballet mistress – in this case Ms Dubois – over the coming months to teach the ballet.

But this was the first time he was addressing the Grade 7s. SABA had never before hosted two separate, full-length ballets for the juniors and seniors.

Gemma, Marley and Dineo were sitting together in the middle of the large group of Grade 7 girls.

The SS were seated right in the front row, as though

being right under Mr Milano's nose might make a difference in the final selection.

"Wow, I can't believe this is actually happening!" Gemma gushed to her friends.

She hadn't slept much last night. Her mind had ditched all thoughts of Emily and Oliver running away with her and conjuring up the most fantastical images of her in a white gauzy dress in the role of Giselle.

Gemma looked over to the boys and could see Ethan and Mitchell talking up a storm with a bunch of other guys. Discussing a TV game of some kind, she thought, by the look of their exaggerated action movie-style movements.

Voices suddenly dropped to low whispers and shhhs echoed around the group as Mr Milano strode across the wooden floor, followed closely by The Banshee who was fanning her face with some papers and muttering something to herself, and then Ms Dubois.

By the time Mr Milano reached the centre of the room, you could hear a pin drop. The sense of anticipation among the students filled every inch of the vast studio.

Mr Milano was older than the other teachers, Gemma guessed, about 60 or so. He was bald on top with a ring of silvery white hair that stood out in little tufts next to his ears and around the back of his head. He always wore the same thing: a white button-up shirt tucked into black slacks and men's dance shoes.

He reminded Gemma of one of those Antarctic penguins with the tufty feathers at the sides of their heads. Although much more agile, of course. The man could still put most of the SABA guys to shame on the stage, tackling everything from *grand jetés* to *fouetté* turns with ease.

He cleared his throat.

"Hello, hello, hello," he said, looking out across the sea of excited faces and smiling warmly.

"Today is a very special day. Not only is this the first time in our history as the South African Ballet Academy that we are hosting two full-length ballets, but the first time that our Grade 7s are performing their own. It took us as the staff faculty a long time to come to that decision, because as you all know, there are many logistics involved in performing a ballet. Many of which come down to me." The old ballet master pulled an "eeek!" face, eliciting a collective laugh from the group.

"However, many of the technical details come down to you." He waved his hand out across the group. "We asked ourselves, 'would our dancers be able to handle such a ballet at this stage?', 'are they technically ready to perform the roles required of them?' and 'are they committed enough to see this ballet through from the very beginning, from today, this moment right now, to the final curtain call?' And we decided that yes, yes you would be able to handle such a massive undertaking because you are one of the strongest Grade 7 groups we have had in at least twenty years at the academy." A soft murmur rippled through the group.

"That means there is a lot of expectation on all of you right now. And today I want to stress the importance of the next three months to not only the school, but to your futures as well. The stand-out performances in this ballet could secure those dancers' future places in the South African National Ballet, or companies beyond our borders."

Gemma grabbed Dineo and Marley's hands, and squeezed hard, looking from one friend to the next. For the first time in her life, Dineo was actually beaming, a huge smile stretching from ear to ear. She was positively elated. Marley looked, well, a little dazed. Gemma realised her friend was completely overwhelmed by the news – a first for her too, as easy-going Marley usually took everything in her stride.

Whispers of "wow" and "oh my gosh" filtered through the group, with girls and boys alike looking at their friends with big, excited eyes.

"Today," Mr Milano began again, the noise level instantly falling away to silence, "is the first day of something special for all of us. I want you to remember that in the weeks ahead. There will be days when balancing everything is going to be difficult, so here is some advice: work hard at your school work and in the studio – give both the right amount of attention, manage your time well, and stay committed. If you can do that, then," he clapped his hands together, bringing them to his chest, "you will succeed. Right?" he nodded to the students to his right, then those in the middle and finally those to his left for emphasis.

"Good!" he stepped back, signally the end of his pep talk and the beginning of business.

Ms Dubois and The Banshee stood up from where

they had been sitting by Mr Rose at the piano. Ms Dubois joined Mr Milano upfront and The Banshee, still furiously fanning herself, said her goodbyes to the teachers before scurrying out the studio.

"Right." Mr Milano's voice cut through group's fervent chatter. "On your feet," he said, raising both hands.

"There are eight main characters in *Giselle*, which means eight major roles. Four of these characters perform solos. We also have three *pas de deux*. Working with a partner can be difficult as it takes two …" The ballet master suddenly swept Ms Dubois up in an impromptu dance, "to tango. So to speak, of course! You both need to be acutely aware of every step, otherwise …" He suddenly spun the petite teacher away from him and as she stumbled, caught her, dipping her low to the ground, "someone could get hurt."

Ms Dubois daintily drew herself back up in first position, and then curtsied to Mr Milano, who laughed heartily as he bowed to her.

"None of you have ever done partner work before, so we'll spend a lot of time on this initially as all three of the primary characters – Giselle and the two men trying to woo her – dance together in *pas de deux* at some stage. Today, we learn the basics," he said, as he began arranging the boys in two lines, shortest to tallest. Ms Dubois did the same to the girls.

For the last two years the Grade 7 girls' height ranking had been the same: Marley in eighth position followed by Gemma, Aimee, Amber, Naledi and Dineo, with the rest of the tallies behind Dineo.

Gemma was too scared to look who she'd be partnered with. Mr Milano was still faffing with the boys, plucking one from here and swapping him with two over there. He stood back and checked the line. "Yes!" he clapped his hands together, "that is good."

Gemma could feel eyes on her, and not just one pair. For a start, Aimee was practically boring a hole into the back of her head. And she could feel the gaze of someone to her right. She slowly looked up and locked eyes with Ethan. He was standing opposite her, a smile creeping over his face. Now Gemma knew why Aimee was having kittens behind her; Gemma had been paired with Ethan.

Gemma felt a stab of insecurity, her nerves twisting in her stomach. She was about to learn one of the most important lessons of her ballet career so far, and she'd been lucky enough to be partnered with a strong dancer like Ethan. She had heard he was a brilliant dancer, and had really impressed the teachers since joining SABA.

Would her dancing be good enough today next to such a talented dancer?

She didn't let on, especially not in front of Aimee. She smiled back at Ethan and turned to face the front.

Mr Milano began to explain the ins and outs of partnering. At first they would do basic exercises so the girls could learn how to transfer their weight with their partners holding them. Then they'd move onto *promenades* and *pirouettes*, finishing off with lifts when the guys were stronger.

Gemma and Ethan, and Marley and Mitch were in the front row with three other couples, and Aimee and

Amber and their partners were directly behind. Naledi and Dineo were further down the second row. Gemma was grateful to have her best friend by her side; it was going to be a long class, all *en pointe*.

She was suddenly aware of Ethan standing behind her. She could feel his warm breath on the back of her neck. Her heart did a nervous flip.

"Core strength is the most important part of partnering, for both partners. Ladies, I want strong trunks," Mr Milano thrust his hands down either side of his own torso. "Tailbones tucked in, no leaning, no caving in. Strong. Gentlemen, I want strong trunks too but also," he slapped his thigh, "strong legs. You are going to support your partner. If you wobble, she wobbles too. Ladies in fifth please and gentlemen in second. Ladies up *en pointe*, arms fifth position *en avant* and stand strong." He raised a clenched fist.

Gemma pulled up easily *en pointe*.

"Gentlemen, hands on either side of your partner's waist." Mr Milano was now behind Ms Dubois. "Not their hips, in the waist," he demonstrated.

Ethan gently placed his hands on Gemma's waist.

"Gentlemen, slowly sway your partners to the left side. Ladies stay strong! And back to the middle. Now to the right side. Ladies your feet stay in the same spot, you're the pendulum in an old grandfather clock, ticking slowly left and then right, left and then right …"

Mr Milano's voice drifted off as Gemma concentrated, engaging all her core muscles to make sure she didn't buckle.

"Now make the swinging action bigger. Gentlemen, move your arms wider part, into second, and gently move your partner from hand to hand, left to right. Watch iiiiit," he said to a couple somewhere behind Gemma. "You're not strong, you're going to fall," he was saying to someone else. The sound of scuffles to Gemma's right told her another girl had come off *pointe*, and then another. "Ladies, stay strong!" Mr Milano reiterated.

Gemma was solid, moving easily from left to right.

Ethan's hands were gentle, but strong on her waist.

"Good!" Mr Milano said, pointing at Gemma and Ethan.

"Yes, nice!" he said to Marley and Mitch.

"I like what I'm seeing here," he said as he walked behind Aimee, Amber and at the end of the row, Dineo.

After thirty minutes of "tick tocking" as Mr Milano called it, they moved onto basic turns. "Gentlemen, stay where you are. Ladies, arms second, legs *développé à la seconde en l'air en pointe*. Now, gentlemen, hold your partners on their forearms and slowly walk around in a circle, turning your partner as you go," he walked around Ms Dubois, turning her a full 360 degrees.

Ethan moved his hands to Gemma's arms and slowly turned her *en pointe*. She couldn't believe it! It was so easy and felt amazing! She caught Marley's eye mid-turn and could see her friend was just as ecstatic.

As she circled towards the back, Gemma also happened to catch Aimee's stare; she was less pleased. In fact, she was downright furious, Gemma could tell. It was either because she'd been paired with Dieter von Horst who was notoriously difficult, or because Gemma had been paired with Ethan. She suspected it was the latter.

They did many more circles, in both directions and on both sides.

"Now, the last one for today is the promenade. We're just going to learn the first steps, but eventually it will look like this," Mr Milano said, moving to stand in front of Ms Dubois, his arms in fourth, crossed, palms facing out.

Ms Dubois stepped forward into *attitude*, her arms also in fourth crossed. As she did, both teachers' hands met at the top and the bottom, Mr Milano supporting her in demi-*pointe*.

He then circled behind her, their arms moving in a graceful circle of their own until Ms Dubois had turned around completely and was facing the front again, but now with her arms resting gently on Mr Milano's forearm, leg still in a perfect *attitude* behind her.

It was such an exquisite, fluid movement, and so flawlessly executed by the two teachers, Gemma found herself lost in the beauty of it.

"For now, I just want you to step towards your partner *en pointe* in the *attitude* and hold hands," Mr Milano explained.

"Ooooh!" someone exclaimed from the back row, prompting a few muffled giggles.

The guys now moved to stand in front of their partners. Ethan's eyes shone with curious excitement.

"Now ladies, step forward towards your partner, gentlemen get ready to receive your partners," the ballet master instructed.

Gemma took a deep breath and stepped up *en pointe*, her arms automatically going to fourth crossed in front of her.

Ethan was ready and caught both her hands securely as she approached.

But Gemma's weight wasn't centred.

She stumbled, lurching forwards towards Ethan.

He quickly released her hands and caught her before she hit the floor.

"Whoa! What's going on here?" Mr Milano asked, rushing over.

Heat instantly flashed across Gemma's face.

She heard Aimee let out a not-so-stifled laugh behind her.

"Are you okay?" Mr Milano put his hand on Gemma's shoulder.

She nodded silently, still trying to process what happened.

"Sorry, it was my fault," Ethan said. "My hands weren't ready."

Gemma looked at him in disbelief.

Ethan looked from Mr Milano to her and back again.

"It won't happen again, sorry," he said, before Gemma could protest.

"Okay," Mr Milano patted Ethan on his shoulder as he walked back to the front of the studio. "You see, like I said, you must be aware of your partner's every step. Let's try again."

"You okay?" Ethan whispered.

Gemma nodded again. She was still a little shaky.

Her mind whirred between almost falling and Ethan covering for her.

Ethan bent his head towards hers. "When you step up, draw up, not forward."

They were back in position again, and Mr Milano gave the order for the girls to move.

Gemma stepped forward, Ethan caught her hands and she held a perfect *attitude en pointe*, supported by Ethan.

"Very good. All of you!" Mr Milano exclaimed. "Right, Mr Rose, give us a waltz please," he added, turning to the old pianist. "I want to see twenty of all three movements on both legs, from the top."

The class ended with Mr Milano showing the dancers the correct way to bow and curtsy to their partners.

Ethan's impish grin returned as he bowed, and Gemma couldn't help but smile back as she curtsied, her earlier embarrassment evaporating.

As dancers scattered to change, Marley and Mitch appeared at Gemma's side.

"Hey, brother, why you trying to kill my bestie?" Marley asked Ethan in a classic Jamaican accent.

Gemma burst out laughing. "It wasn't really …" she started to say.

"Yes, sorry about that," Ethan interrupted. "I don't know what happened. Won't happen again. Promise," he put his right hand on his heart and his left in the air like he was taking an oath.

Gemma didn't know why Ethan had taken the blame

for her mistake. She was grateful he had, she'd been embarrassed enough as it was, but he could mess up his chances with Mr Milano. She realised the sacrifice he had made.

"Thanks," she said earnestly to Ethan. "I appreciate what you did. And thanks for the advice too."

"No problem, Gemma, any time," he smiled.

The girls headed back to the dorms to change for lunch and afternoon classes, excitedly comparing notes the whole way about their first *pas de deux* class.

Like Gemma, Marley was stoked, and said Mitch was an excellent partner.

Dineo was satisfied, but really thought Mr Milano should have let them complete the *promenades*.

"We're ready for it, I'm telling you," she said.

"Baby steps, Neo, baby steps!" Marley tickled her friend in the ribs. "We can't all be instant pros at partnering," she teased.

Gemma was grateful they hadn't mentioned her near fall. They seemed to have bought Ethan's story. She knew she always said he was a nice guy, but she was starting to see just how true that was.

"How your toes feeling after that, Gems?" Marley asked.

"Actually pretty good. I soaked them and used double… Oh no!" She stopped abruptly. "I left my toe caps behind! I need to go back to the studio and get them. I'll see you at lunch!" she called over her shoulder as she raced back to the studio.

When she got there, Mr Rose and Mr Milano were discussing the music for *Giselle*.

"Such a beautiful ballet," Mr Rose was saying, "the second act with the lake has always been my favourite. Reminds me of the lake right here at Forestlake Estate ..."

"But without the wilis, of course!" Mr Milano chuckled.

Gemma spotted her toe caps in the corner where she'd taken off her shoes. She walked over and bent down to pick them up.

"Ah, but we have our own lake spirits, don't we now? That's Oliver's favourite spot, remember?"

Gemma stopped. Had she just heard right? Lake spirits, Oliver ... She couldn't believe her ears. She had to tell the others! She grabbed her toe caps and sprinted out the studio back towards the dorms.

Marley had already changed and left for lunch, her ballet clothes lying in a crumpled heap on the floor. Gemma tore off her own clothes as quickly as she could; she had to tell Marley what she'd heard. They had to go back and speak to Mr Rose.

She pulled on her uniform and knelt down to tie her school shoes. Something on the floor caught her eye. She looked closer; it was a letter that had been slipped under the door.

She picked it up. It had her name on the front: GEMMA in big thick red capitals.

She opened the letter. "I know you were out the other night. With two boys. I saw you and I'm going to tell. You can kiss your part in *Giselle* goodbye."

Chapter 6

"You know who wrote this, of course?" Marley was sitting across from Gemma at the lunch table, the note in her hands.

"Yup," Gemma nodded slowly.

Dineo was reading the note over Marley's shoulder. "She's really got it in for you."

"Yup."

"And you know why?" Marley asked again.

"I do. It's because of yesterday, because I got paired with Ethan."

"More like because she can see Ethan likes you and she wants him all to herself," Marley said.

"Well, I really don't think it's like that. Ethan is just a nice guy. I mean, he's nice to everybody, even Aimee, for goodness sake! But she doesn't know that. She does think it's just about me. So she's bringing out the big guns," Gemma said.

"What are you going to do? The production means everything to you, you can't allow this to ruin it." Dineo was genuinely concerned for her friend.

"It's not going to," Gemma said. "Remember last year when we went to watch *Swan Lake* at the Nelson

73

Mandela Theatre?"

"Oh yes! I'd forgotten all about that! Brilliant!" Marley was nodding excitedly.

Last year, the juniors had been given a day pass to attend the visiting Imperial Russian Ballet's performance of *Swan Lake*. It was at the beginning of scene four that Gemma needed to go to the bathroom. As she dashed across the theatre lobby, she saw a fancy chauffeur-driven Mercedes-Benz pull up outside. Certain that it was somebody famous, she ducked behind the *Swan Lake* cardboard cut-out by the ticket counter and waited to see who it was. Aimee and Amber emerged from the car carrying two large tog bags and, looking rather guilty, secretly let themselves back into the theatre. That night at dinner, the girls overheard Aimee and Amber bragging about their recent acquisitions from a designer clothing sale in Sandton. They didn't, of course, say how they'd gotten their fancy new heels, bags and jeans. Sneaking out of the school grounds or while on a school outing was a serious offence.

Dineo's frown deepened. "Aimee will just say she didn't do it, and Amber will back her up?"

"There are little things at the theatre called security cameras, and one points right at the entrance doors. If I need proof, I've got it."

"Well I think you are going to need it." Dineo was watching the SS girls at their table two rows down. Aimee had her eyes fixed on Gemma, a look of absolute satisfaction on her face.

Gemma turned in her chair to follow Dineo's gaze,

and caught Aimee's stare.

Aimee folded her arms across her chest, sat back in her chair and raised an eyebrow, challenging Gemma.

Gemma gave her a "whatever" shrug, and turned back to face her friends.

"Are you going to talk to her, tell her what you've got on her?" Marley asked.

"Nope. I'm just going to leave it. She'll soon see Ethan's just a friend, and when she does, she'll be more focused on trying to get him than trying to get me," Gemma said, taking a huge bite of her spaghetti bolognaise.

"Wouldn't it be better just to tell her now and get it out the way?" Dineo asked.

"No. I think we need to beat her at her own game. Let her think she really has something on me and then take her down at the last minute. She's never going to leave us alone otherwise," Gemma said in between mouthfuls.

"Dangerous game, Gems," Dineo said. "I'd just tell her, get it over with, and leave her and the ghost alone."

"Oh, I forgot to tell you!" Gemma grabbed Marley's hand across the table. "You'll never believe what I heard when I went back to the studio. Mr Rose and Mr Milano were talking about *Giselle*, and Mr Rose said 'we have our own lake spirits, the lake is Oliver's favourite spot'!"

Marley stared at Gemma in disbelief. "Are you serious?

"Yes!" she was now shaking Marley's arm excitedly. "We have to speak to him tomorrow after practice!"

The next morning, Gemma could feel little bubbles of excitement gurgling through her system. Not only because she was going to learn the next steps in partnering, but because they were finally going to find out more about Oliver.

The morning's classes passed relatively hassle-free, except for English, where Aimee deliberately bumped into Gemma in the line outside class.

"Oh sorry," she said looking down her nose at Gemma. "I didn't see you there. Must be because you're always sneaking around in the dark."

"Oh bite me," Gemma said, unmoved by Aimee's dig at her.

"Ag," Aimee muttered, stalking off to the back of the line.

Gemma ignored Aimee's stares during school, and in ballet class that afternoon where they became insanely crazy when Mr Milano said the students had to keep the same partners as the day before.

"Hi." Ethan smiled brightly as he approached Gemma.

"Hey!" she smiled back. She felt her tummy lurch. Damn nerves, she thought. She took a deep breath; she was determined to get everything right today.

Mr Milano clapped his hands and called the class to attention.

"Today we'll be doing the same as yesterday. First we tick tock, starting small, and getting wider, wider, wider. Then we do turns, both sides, and then we do the first part of the promenade. Remember, I want to see strong bodies." He made a fist for emphasis. "Mr Rose …"

The piano began, and Gemma rose up strongly *en pointe*. Ethan's hands were steady and caught her waist. She moved from left to right, keeping her weight evenly balanced and constantly pulling up her body through her feet to the top of her head. She was focused, strong.

Mr Milano nodded his approval as he walked past. As he gave the cue for the next exercise, Gemma switched effortlessly into the turns, her arms moving into second, her right leg floating up into a *développé à la seconde en l'air en pointe* without missing a beat.

Ethan was perfectly in tune with Gemma, and immediately moved his arms to her forearm and began circling around her, turning her at the same time.

Gemma was always acutely aware of every movement. While some girls danced on autopilot, Gemma never did. She thought about every move and how to perfectly execute it every time. Now she felt how she had to centre her weight as Ethan turned her so she wouldn't fall, all while pulling up through her body.

Gemma and Ethan flowed from the turns into the first part of the promenade, Gemma stepping up into the *attitude*, Ethan holding her hands in fourth.

Mr Milano explained how the boys had to gently turn their partners now as they moved behind them, their arms circling around twice so the girls spun around *en pointe*, and eventually ended up facing the front again, in *attitude*, their arms resting gently on their partners' forearms.

Instinct seemed to take over. As Ethan moved behind Gemma, her arms circled around, she intuitively adjusted her weight as she moved into the turn and was suddenly facing the front in *attitude*. It was perfect, she knew it was.

Mr Milano smiled approvingly. They did 10 more complete *promenades*, each one a little better than the one before. Gemma was ecstatic! One of the most technically challenging movements she'd ever learnt and she'd nailed it!

Gemma was on an absolute high by the time Mr Milano dismissed the class with strict instructions for all students to brush up on their *Giselle* knowledge. Her heart felt light and happy.

"You're really good, you know," Ethan said to Gemma as she began to make her way towards Marley and Dineo.

"Oh, thanks," she said. Nobody else had ever told Gemma she was good before. Of course her mom and her dad did, and her friends, but not other people who didn't know her. Not people who were really good themselves, like Ethan. It made her feel even more amazing. By the time Gemma reached her friends, she was floating on a pink puffy cloud of ballet happiness.

"Ready to go chat to Mr Rose?" Marley asked Gemma excitedly as she approached. "I told the boys to come too."

"Oh yes!" Gemma exclaimed. She'd been so caught up in her own excitement, she'd forgotten completely about quizzing the old pianist.

"Can we meet at the summerhouse at 3pm?" Dineo asked, slinging her bag over her shoulder. "I thought we could go through the *Giselle* book I took out of the library this morning?"

"Good idea, Neo! Yes, we'll see you later!" Gemma said.

Marley filled Mitch and Ethan in on the conversation Gemma had overheard the day before, and the four of them set off to speak to Mr Rose. He was merrily humming away to himself as he gathered up some music sheets from the small wooden table next to his piano when they arrived.

"Mr Rose, can we please talk to you for a minute?" Gemma asked as the group approached him.

He turned around, still humming. A broad smile lit up his small round face with its rosy red cheeks.

"Of course, my dear, what can I do for you wonderful young people today?" he asked happily.

Gemma had a soft spot for Mr Rose. He was always so friendly and kind, and he loved being around the students. He said it kept him young.

"We wanted to know if you knew anything about Oliver Black, the original caretaker's son who used to live here?" Gemma asked.

Mr Rose nodded as she spoke.

"Hmmm, now there's a story. A damn shame too," he said shaking his head. "Such a wonderful young lad taken too soon," he said staring out the window, lost in thought.

"Did you know his family?" Ethan asked.

"No, no I didn't sonny, but an old friend of mine who lived in the same street as Oliver and his father knew the Black family. They always said he was a good boy, always helped his father and did them proud. Took his own life, he did. Right here in this very school. But nobody knew why. My friend told me Oliver's family said he was always such a happy boy, and he had just gotten married too, you know," the old man shook his head again.

"You said he died here, at the school?" Gemma gently probed.

"Oh yes, yes he did. He walked into the lake, just like that. But he couldn't swim, and he drowned," Mr Rose said.

Gemma wondered if Clarence had had something to do with Oliver's death. "How do you know he took his own life and somebody else wasn't responsible?"

"They say his father saw him. He was working in the gardens when he saw Oliver walking into the water. He called out to him to stop, but the boy just kept on walking, deeper and deeper into the water. By the time his father reached the edge of the lake, Oliver was gone. No sign of him. Such a tragedy," Mr Rose said softly.

"Sometimes people who die so tragically don't fully leave the place of their death. Do you know if Oliver has ever ...uh... been seen around campus?" Marley asked.

"Oh! You mean his ghost? Yes dearie, yes he has. Some years on the anniversary of his death he has been seen, just down there by the water's edge." He pointed out the window to the forest that lay beyond the sports field. "I believe his spirit is still here. Like you say dearie, he hasn't fully left this place, bound to it by the awful circumstances that made him take his own life. I suppose we'll never know why." Mr Rose stared out the window again.

"Have you ever seen his ghost?" Mitch asked.

"Oh no, not me laddie. I keep well away from those parts. There are old stories that tell of magic in that forest. Strange things happen there. Poor old Oliver is not the only being that haunts these parts I tell you," Mr Rose said earnestly.

Gemma felt the hairs on her arms stand up. As if Forestlake Estate didn't have enough secrets already. She looked from Mr Rose to the forest beyond and wondered what other mysteries the ancient trees there had concealed beneath their dark leafy canopy.

"If that's all, I must be off now dearies," Mr Rose said, sliding his sheet music into a well-worn brown leather satchel and threading the straps through two silver buckles.

"Thank you, Mr Rose," Gemma said.

"My pleasure my dear, my pleasure," he said shuffling off towards the door. "Oh," he suddenly stopped in the arched doorway of the studio and turned to face them. "You children be careful now if you plan to venture into that dark wood," he said more seriously. He nodded to himself before turning for the door again. "Bye bye dearies," he lifted his hand in a half-wave as he shuffled off.

"Wow!" Gemma said, her eyes glistening with excitement as she looked around the group. "So now we know what happened to Oliver. And where to find him."

"What we don't know is how to bring those two together so they can sort out their lovers' quarrel," Ethan offered.

81

"Shoot," Gemma looked at her watch. "We need to meet Dineo now. We're going through *Giselle* like Mr Milano said, to better understand the story behind the ballet." "Do you guys want to come too?" Marley asked.

"Yes sirreee!" said Mitch, clicking his heels together and standing to attention.

"Cool. If you don't mind us tagging along?" Ethan asked.

"Nope, that's cool," Gemma replied as Marley linked arms with her and marched them off towards the door, with Mitch and Ethan trailing behind.

Dineo was already sitting in the summerhouse paging through the *Giselle* book.

"Uncovered anything interesting yet?" Gemma asked, hopping up onto the seat next to her and peering over Dineo's shoulder.

"It's quite a technical ballet. We'll have to work hard for the leads, that's for sure," Dineo said, leafing back through the pages to beginning of the book.

"What's the story actually about?" Ethan asked. "I just know there's a part where Giselle goes mad or something?"

"Well, the story is about a young girl who lives in a village with her mother. She was the prettiest girl in the village, and the best dancer too. She meets a guy and they fall in love …"

"Whoa, but not just any guy," Gemma interrupted. "It says here he was the prince, but he was dressed like just a regular guy so that nobody would recognise him."

"Yes, because he was actually already engaged to be married," Dineo continued. "So the prince, Albrecht was

82

his name, snuck into a cottage in the village, changed into ordinary clothes and he would then visit Giselle. Albrecht was helped by his loyal servant Wilfred, and even changed his name to Loys so that nobody would know he was really the prince."

Gemma was reading ahead. "But it looks like somebody else liked Giselle already – a guy called Hilarion?"

"Yup," said Dineo. "It says here he was from the village like Giselle, and he also loved her. He was a game ranger, and led hunting trips in the nearby forest. He used to get really angry when Loys would come to the village, because Giselle would spend all her time dancing with him, and just ignore Hilarion. This upset Hilarion, who suspected Loys was up to no good. He even told Giselle not to trust Loys, but she said she loved him, so she didn't listen."

"Whoa!" Gemma exclaimed, almost falling over Dineo to read the next part. "But then a hunting party arrived in the village one day, and one of the people with them was the princess that Loys ... uh, Prince Albrecht, was supposed to marry! In the meantime, Hilarion went to the cottage where Albrecht used to change into his Loys clothes, and saw Albrecht's royal clothes and sword. He figures out Loys is actually Albrecht, and rats him out in front of the entire hunting party and the princess."

"At which point the princess confirms Loys is actually Prince Albrecht, and they are due to be married. This is where Giselle goes mad," Dineo looked up at Ethan.

She read the next part out loud: "Giselle is devastated

by the news and completely overcome by grief. She simply cannot believe what Loys has done, how he has deceived her. She dances wildly, as though trying to find a way to deal with the pain of what has happened, but it is all too much for her."

"Ah," Gemma gasped, clasping her hand over her mouth. "She died. She collapsed while dancing and died. Of a broken heart."

"Wow," Ethan said flatly. "That's hectic. Sounds a lot like Emily, hey? She died of a broken heart too."

"And she was a dancer. And she felt she was deceived by Oliver, because she believed he'd run off with someone else and never loved her," Marley added.

"Ah!" Gemma gasped again. "And look here, Giselle becomes a ghost after her death too. She also doesn't rest in peace, just like Emily!"

"No way!" Marley and Mitchell said in unison.

Ethan's eyes were big "Are you serious?"

"Yes! It says right there that in the forest that bordered the village where Giselle lived was a group of spirits called the wilis. They were the ghosts of the girls whose loves had left them before they could marry. And they haunted the forest looking for guys to get their revenge on. When Giselle died, they summoned her spirit to join them in their quest. So she becomes a ghost in the second act of the ballet," Gemma said excitedly.

Ethan's eyes widened. "This is seriously creepy!"

"How does the story end?" Mitch asked. "Maybe there are clues there we could like, follow, to help Emily?"

Dineo picked up the story. "Like Gemma said, the

wilis held a grudge against all mortal men. The villa͟ᵍ
knew this and wouldn't stray into the forest at night. For
it was there, in the moonlit glades, that the wilis would
seek out men who had wandered into the forest or maybe
gotten lost among the trees, and exact their revenge on
them by surrounding them and dancing with them until
they became exhausted and eventually died."

Ethan was incredulous. "They danced the guys to
death?"

"Yes, yes these sylph-like spirits used to come out
at night when the village clock struck midnight, and
glide around the forest looking for their victims. They
were led by a cruel queen called Myrtha who showed no
mercy. But when the clock chimed four in the morning,
the wilis would return to their graves until the following
night when they would wait for their next victims.

A few nights after Giselle is buried, Hilarion leads a
hunting party into the forest. They stay too late in the
forest and it's soon near midnight. Hilarion sees Giselle's
grave, and other graves too, and tells his guests they have
stumbled into an area known to be haunted by wilis. The
forest is cold, dark and eerie, and the hunting party flees
in alarm. Hilarion lingers a moment at Giselle's grave.
Suddenly the village clock chimes midnight. Hilarion is
no longer alone: Myrtha, Queen of the wilis, rises from
her slumber. Hilarion takes off in fright.

Myrtha summonses the other wilis, and soon the
forest is filled with spirits gliding around the glade in a
wild dance, their wispy dresses shimmering silver in the
moonlight. Queen Myrtha commands that Giselle, the

newest wili, rises from her grave. Giselle joins her new sisters in their ethereal dance.

But then someone else enters the scene. It's Prince Albrecht. He is devastated by Giselle's death for he truly loved her. He brings with him a wreath to lay at her grave. He got lost in the forest, so has arrived too late, and doesn't realise the clock has chimed midnight and the wilis are about. He places the wreath by her grave and is so lost in his grief, doesn't see the wilis silently circling around him. When he does look up, he sees Giselle's spirit in front of him. At first she teases him, disappearing and then reappearing again, but once the other wilis have danced away to another part of the glade, Giselle dances with Prince Albrecht. This is one of the most difficult *pas de deux.*" Dineo broke away from the story to see a circle of eager faces staring back. "It's very difficult to perform, with some ..."

"Ooooh, Neo, the story! We want to know what happens in the story!" Gemma said eagerly.

Dineo sighed loudly. "Okay. I was just saying. So then the two of them dance, unaware that the reason why the other wilis have left them alone is because they have stumbled upon Hilarion. Giselle's other love has returned to the forest alone this time to pay his last respects at her graveside. But the wilis' power has already taken effect and Hilarion is caught up in their wild dance. Soon he's exhausted and begs for mercy, but the spirits keep dancing and eventually he collapses to the ground. They pick up his body and toss it into the lake.

The wilis know Prince Albrecht is there, and come

for him too. Giselle is frantic, she knows what the wilis will do if they get near Prince Albrecht, and out of her love for him she tells him to hang onto the cross that watches over her grave. Myrtha cannot command Albrecht to dance while he clutches the cross. The evil queen comes up with a new plan: she commands Giselle to dance around Albrecht to tempt him away from the cross. Giselle cannot fight the queen's magic, and she does as she is commanded. Soon Albrecht lets go of the cross, and begins to dance with Giselle.

It's not long before Giselle sees the prince is near death. She realises that she still loves him, and has forgiven him for what he did to her. So she tries to protect him by dancing more slowly despite the queen's protests. Her ploy works, and suddenly the village clock strikes 4am. The queen has no more power over Giselle, and all the wilis return their graves. Prince Albrecht is saved. He collapses in a crumpled heap on the forest floor.

But Giselle hasn't only saved her prince, she has saved herself as well. By defying her own nature as a wili – one intent on killing Albrecht – and showing him only love, Giselle has broken the curse on herself too. She disappears, back to the sanctuary of her grave, but as a spirit at peace. She is no longer a wili. And Prince Albrecht is left weeping at her grave as he finally realises the magnitude of Giselle's love for him. And that's how it ends," Dineo said, slapping the book shut.

Dineo looked up to see Gemma, Marley, Mitch and Ethan completely spellbound by the enchanted story.

"It's forgiveness. That's the key," Gemma said slowly,

her mind working quickly to make the connections. "That's what finally released Giselle from the wilis' spell and let her rest in peace – forgiving Albrecht, and having the chance to show him that."

"Maybe if Emily is given the chance to tell Oliver that she forgives him, she can let go too and will also rest in peace?" Ethan ventured.

"Yes! That makes perfect sense!" Marley enthused. "Forgiveness is a means of release for spirits. Once they forgive, or know they have been forgiven by the person they hurt, then their work here is done."

"That means the same is true for Oliver," Ethan thought out loud. "I bet that's what keeps him trapped down at the lake; he can't rest in peace because he doesn't have Emily's forgiveness. He can never forgive himself for what he did to her, just like you said, Gemma, that she couldn't forgive herself for feeling responsible for his death."

"So they probably feel responsible for each other's death, and that's what's holding them here?" Mitch said simply.

"Yes, I think that's it!" Gemma nodded. "So just like Giselle and Albrecht had to be together again for Giselle to show him that she had forgiven him, we need to somehow get Emily and Oliver together. So we don't just need to find Oliver, we need to reunite him with Emily."

"So why can't we just tell Emily to go down there, find Oliver and you know, talk to him?" Ethan asked.

"Well Mr Rose says he has only been seen on the anniversary of his death, and that's still two weeks away, on 31 October. Then there's Emily. We know she can get out through the hole in the wall into the rest of the school now, but she can only get out of the building and onto the grounds on the night of 31 October too," Gemma said thoughtfully.

"So that's our night then. That's the night we have to get Emily and get her down to the lake where, hopefully, we'll find Oliver," Ethan said.

"You do realise that 31 October is Halloween, right?" Dineo spoke up for the first time since finishing the story of *Giselle*.

Gemma's eyes widened with excitement. "Oh my word, of course!"

"Wow!" Marley said, shaking her head. "That's just so … wow!"

"What?" the others asked.

"Halloween. That's supposed to be the night when the veil between the physical world and the spiritual world is thinnest," Marley explained. "That's why in the old days they believed supernatural things happened on that night. There couldn't be a better night to conduct a ghostly rescue mission than that night!"

"Then it has to work. Because if it doesn't, we have to wait a whole year before we can try again," Ethan said more seriously. "We only have one shot at this, so we're going to need a fail-proof rescue plan."

"That just leaves the problem of how to devise such a plan," Marley said.

Gemma pulled a face. "And the very big problem of how we're going to get out of the school that night to pull it off."

Chapter 7

It was late on a Thursday afternoon and Gemma was in the studio going through some of the new *Giselle* routines by herself.

The last two weeks had been intense. With the end-of-year academic exams around the corner the teachers were piling on the work, and with the production just five weeks away, ballet classes were equally tough.

The girls and guys were taking separate classes in the morning as they learnt different pieces of the ballet, from the harvest scene in the beginning where all the men and women in the village did different dances, to the specific group work like the arrival of the hunting party in the village and the dance of the wilis.

In the afternoon the guys and girls trained together, learning *pas de deux* routines and strengthening the muscles they needed for these technical partner combinations.

Gemma had thrown herself into the schedule. She worked hard in class, pushing herself to her limit and then, like today, visited the studios in the afternoon to practise some more.

The same way she knew they had just one shot to reunite Emily and Oliver, she also knew she had one shot to impress her teachers and land a solo role.

It wasn't only Gemma's schedule that was unrelenting, Aimee was too.

Aside from the snide remarks she dropped into *pas de deux* training every chance she got – she still hated the fact that Gemma got to train with Ethan every day – she'd begun stalking Gemma too. Well, that was what it felt like.

"You know, everywhere we go, she's there. Her and the rest of the SS, they keep on popping up. I swear they're tracking our every move," Marley said to Gemma one day.

"I know, Amber even followed me to the toilet yesterday, can you believe that?" Gemma asked. "She's trying to catch me out; waiting for me to slip up so she can use it against me."

"And making sure you're not with Ethan," Marley reminded her.

Gemma shrugged. "Maybe."

"She's obsessed with the guy! Last week when I was helping Ms Dubois carry the props from the storeroom, I saw her and Amber walk past Ethan and Mitch like five times! He didn't even notice her. Eventually she actually had to say hello to him just to get him to look up. And then yesterday she 'tripped' in front of him. Being the nice guy he is, he helped her up of course," Marley said.

"Why do you think she hasn't reported you to The Banshee yet?" Dineo asked.

"She's waiting. Waiting for the right time to pounce and really make a scene, I suspect. She'd love to see me go down before the production so I don't get a part in it. The closer we get to curtain up, the better chance she has of that wish coming true. But I won't let her, not this time," Gemma said.

"Just don't jeopardise your chances for a role in *Giselle*. It's not worth it," Dineo had warned.

She was not going to jeopardise anything, Gemma thought now as she prepared for a series of *chaînés* turns on the diagonal. Quietly, neatly, she whipped across the floor, finishing in a perfect *arabesque*.

Slow, deliberate clapping echoed off the empty studio walls.

"Bravo! Bravo!" Aimee's voice dripped sarcasm. She'd snuck into the studio and was standing at the entrance, leaning against the door jamb. "It's so encouraging to see you training so hard, Gems. But you really are wasting your time, you know that right? You'll never get a lead. Or a solo. Not in this lifetime," she said, striding purposefully across the floor towards Gemma. "I just thought I should pop in and say I haven't forgotten about your little evening sojourn the other night. You and your little friends. I don't know what you're up to, but you're going to have to make your move soon. If you don't, I'll go straight to Babington," she said stopping in front of Gemma.

"You don't scare me, Aimee," Gemma stared her squarely in the eyes. "And I don't have to make any move. You think you've got so much dirt on me, tell

Babington. What are you waiting for?"

Aimee regarded her sceptically. She couldn't believe Gemma wasn't going to take the bait, wasn't going to beg her not to tell and wasn't going to plead for a compromise.

"Seriously? You're not even going to fight me on this? You're just going to roll over and play dead? Where's the fun in that? No, sweetie, it's not going to go that way. You," she stabbed her finger in Gemma's chest, "have something I want and you," she stabbed her again, "are going to give it to me. Don't and I'll make your life a living hell. Oh, and I'll still tell Babington, so you're screwed either way," Aimee sneered.

Gemma had something she wanted? That was impossible.

"What do you want that I have?" she asked defiantly.

"Ethan."

Gemma let out a laugh. "I don't have Ethan. We're friends. He's a nice guy, and obviously likes nice girls, and that's why he's my friend. You should try being nice sometime and see where it gets you," Gemma turned to walk away but Aimee grabbed her arm, pulling her back to face her.

"I'm serious. That lead role is mine, and it's pretty obvious Ethan's going to get the role of Prince Albrecht. You see, we're destined to be together on the stage. And off the stage. But you're in our way. Get out of it or I'll make you," Aimee's eyes flashed with anger.

Gemma could feel Aimee's jealousy, it danced around her like fire, burning anyone who dared come too close.

But Gemma meant what she said. The last few weeks of ballet training had made her feel more confident in herself and stronger, both on the outside as a dancer and on the inside as a person. For the first time ever, Gemma truly wasn't scared of Aimee. She'd found her power and she was going to use it.

But her training had also taught her discipline; wasn't ballet all about discipline? Today that discipline meant not playing her hand. It meant keeping her secret about Aimee safe, because she knew one day soon, she was going to have to dish the dirt on the little princess and she was going to need all the ammunition she could get.

"We'll see about that. Now if you don't mind," Gemma pulled free of Aimee's grasp and walked to the back of the studio. By the time she'd turned to prep for another round of *chaînés* turns, the studio was empty. Aimee was gone.

"OMG she actually confessed that this whole thing is about her liking Ethan, and being jealous of you? And that for once, she can't get the guy she likes just by snapping her fingers?" Marley said in utter disbelief the next morning over breakfast.

Dineo was less impressed. "I can't believe she grabbed you like that."

"Oh I know exactly what you three will be going to the ball as," Aimee mocked from behind them. "Yourselves!" she cackled as she slapped a flyer down on the cafeteria table in front of them.

SA Ballet Academy presents the centenary
Masked Halloween Ball!
Come dressed as your favourite masked ghost or
ghoul (or similar character) on 31 October.
Unmasking takes place at 11pm.
Don't miss it!

"Oh, you hadn't heard about the dance yet, had you?" Aimee was now standing in front of Gemma, Marley and Dineo, with Amber and Naledi just behind her. "Of course not, you're always the last to know everything. But don't worry, I'm here to keep you up to speed." She leaned forward, Gemma could feel Aimee's breath on her face. "The school is holding its first ever masked ball, to celebrate its centenary. And we can bring dates. The only thing is," Aimee faked a yawn, "I'm bored with all the boys in this place. But then I remembered you know a guy who would be perfect."

"Why don't you just ask Ethan yourself?" Gemma asked.

Aimee feigned shock, clutching her heart. "Me, ask a guy for something? Puleeze. I never ask boys for anything, let alone dates. Ethan will be my date that night," she said standing upright again. "And you're going to make sure of it." With that she turned on her heel and marched off, with Amber and Naledi scampering behind her.

Gemma shook her head. "She's insane."

"You got that right!" Marley laughed. "Order up! Straitjacket for table 3!" she said perfectly imitating a crackly restaurant kitchen loudspeaker.

Dineo clicked her tongue. "She has a lot of nerve."

"Ag, never mind crazy over there," Gemma motioned in Aimee's direction, "what about this masked ball?" she said excitedly, picking up the flyer Aimee had left behind.

"I know, SABA hasn't held a dance in years!" Marley gushed.

"Oh my word, it couldn't be more perfect …" Gemma suddenly said.

"Uh huh, I know that look. What now?" Marley asked hesitantly.

Gemma tapped the flyer with her finger. "The date – 31 October. Emily … Oliver …?"

Marley caught Gemma's train of thought. "Oh! Yes! The perfect cover for us to execute the rescue mission!"

"There'll be so much going on that night, we should be able to easily slip out and get back by 11pm for the unmasking," Gemma said.

"That's brilliant!" Marley agreed. "Let's meet the guys later so we can figure out all the details."

After their last class, and just before Gemma slipped off to the studio, she and Marley wandered down to the summerhouse. Ethan and Mitch were already there.

"Hey!" Gemma said cheerfully, bouncing up the stairs.

"Bonjour mademoiselle Gemma, mademoiselle Marley," Mitch said flexing the bit of French he knew and air-kissing Gemma and then Marley on both cheeks.

The girls dissolved into giggles.

Ethan laughed too. "Hi guys! So you've got a plan for us?"

"Sort of. You've heard about the Halloween Ball, right?" Gemma asked. The boys nodded. "So we thought we'd all dress in black, wear our masks and slip out at about 9 or so. Then, this is the part we haven't figured out yet, we get Emily, go to the lake, hopefully find Oliver, reunite them and then go back to the ball before we're missed. We can keep in touch with Dineo on her phone to make sure no one's onto us. What do you think?"

"Are we going to have to go to the old studio first to get Emily? That could take quite a while, plus we could easily get bust being in that part of the school when everybody is in the ballroom," Mitch said.

"That's true. Emily can get out of the school building on the anniversary of her death, so maybe she needs to meet us somewhere, like in the garden maybe?" Ethan offered.

"Yup, that could work," Gemma agreed. "But how are we going to get out of the ballroom?"

They all thought for a minute.

"We'll have to create a diversion," Mitch said.

Gemma smiled. She knew Mitch loved action movies. He was always acting out scenes from them, so of course he'd know about diversions and throwing people off your trail.

Ethan shrugged. "We could ask Brent and Zack to help out? They're cool and they won't ask for details.

Maybe they could distract whoever's at the main door and we sneak out the side entrance?"

"The side door will probably be locked," Marley said thoughtfully.

Gemma nodded. "That's true. What if they create their diversion at the main door and we slip through right next to them?"

Ethan rubbed his hands together. "Oooh, risky! Brent and Zack will love that! I'll ask them later."

"Cool, so we kind of have a plan," Mitch confirmed.

Gemma was keen to get back to the studio. "Awesome! I kind of need to go. Chat to you guys later?"

"Adios, ladies," Mitch said.

The girls were halfway down the stairs when Ethan spoke. "Uh, Gemma, could I talk to you quick?" he asked.

Marley raised her eyebrows and grinned at Gemma.

"Sure," she said stopping mid-step on the stairs. She turned around to see Ethan still in the summerhouse and Mitch heading towards her, a huge smile on his face.

She bounded up the stairs back into the summerhouse. "What's up?" she asked nonchalantly.

Ethan swept his long fringe out of his face. His ice-blue eyes shone with excitement, his trademark grin tugging at the corners of his mouth.

"I, um, I was wondering if you had a date for the Halloween Ball?" he asked.

Gemma hadn't even thought about a date for the ball!

"No I don't," she said.

"Would you maybe like to go with me?" he ventured cautiously.

What? He wants to go to the ball with me?

Gemma felt heat creep across her cheeks and her heart quicken.

Ethan smiled at her, arching one eyebrow. "And so?"

"Oh, um, yes! Yes, I'd love to!" she said laughing, embarrassed at how lost she'd been in her thoughts.

Ethan's smile broadened. "Great!"

Gemma had been caught so off-guard, her mind was still whirling. "Um, I need to, um, go. To the studio," she quickly clarified. "To, uh, practice," she bumbled. What on earth was wrong with her? She couldn't even talk properly.

Ethan let out a little laugh. "Ok cool. I'll see you in class tomorrow?"

Gemma nodded, a smile forcing its way through her confusion.

She turned and high-tailed it down the stairs to Marley, who was laughing at a joke Mitch had just told her. Seeing Gemma approaching, Mitch waved goodbye to Marley, and then dashed back up the stairs towards Ethan.

"Bye Gems!" he called as he passed her.

"So?" Marley prompted.

"He asked me to go to the ball with him!" Gemma whispered excitedly.

Marley fell in step alongside Gemma, linking her arm through Gemma's. "And?"

"Well of course I said yes!" Gemma whispered again.

"I knew it! I told you Gems. You see, your best friend always knows best!" Marley squeezed Gemma in a side hug. "Mitch asked me too," she beamed.

"What?" Gemma stopped, a huge smile on her face. "That's awesome Marls!"

"Pretty cool, hey?"

"Totally! Mitch is such a great guy!"

"He is. He's been making me laugh so much that my stomach hurts! So how does it feel to officially be asked out by the cutest junior in the school?"

"Um, I'm still processing that!" Gemma laughed. Although she'd never thought of Ethan as anything more than just a friend, being asked out for the first time ever by a guy like him made her feel giddy.

That afternoon Gemma could barely concentrate on her routines. Her heart felt like it had little wings on either side that were fluttering non-stop in her chest, and if it could, it would suddenly take flight and fly away. And she had a happy little smile stuck on her face that lasted all afternoon and was still there when she drifted off to dreamland that night.

Gemma was still on cloud nine the next morning, but she felt her stomach sink when Dineo told her and Marley that The Banshee would be taking their class that morning.

"Apparently Ms Dubois is sick and Mr Milano is working with the guys, so she has to take it," Dineo shrugged, pulling off her sweat pants. "And I believe she's in a foul mood because of it. I think we should warm up earlier today," she said, putting her *pointe* shoes on.

"Good idea," Marley agreed, rummaging in her bag for her shoes.

Gemma felt the flutter of her heart change from the ecstasy of Ethan's proposal to the dread of The Banshee's cold hard stare and impatient way. She hurriedly opened her bag to put on her own *pointe* shoes. She automatically felt down the left side where they always were, but came up empty handed. Gemma frowned. That was strange, they were always there. She opened the bag wider and looked inside. She couldn't see her *pointe* shoe bag. At all.

"What's wrong?" Marley asked Gemma.

"My shoes. They're gone," Gemma said, her frown deepening.

"What do you mean they're gone? Did you leave them here last night maybe?" Dineo asked, looking instantly concerned for her friend.

"No, they were here last night when I took my other pair out to pancake them," Gemma said, emptying the contents of her bag onto the floor. Three spare leotards, two packets of new tights, leg warmers, waistbands, hair clips and nets, and two bottles of La Pebra's fell out, but no shoes.

Dineo's eyes were big. "Did you say you pancaked your other pair last night? So they're not here either?"

"Uh huh," Gemma was frantically checking through everything again, inside her pockets of her bag, the outside zip pocket. Nothing.

Just then The Banshee walked into the studio, clapping her hands to bring everyone to attention. "Come, come girls," she said as she strutted across the front of the studio.

Gemma felt hot and cold all over at the same time. Her hands began to shake.

"Here," Dineo whispered, thrusting one of her spare pairs of pointes under Gemma's nose. "Take these. Hurry!"

Dineo and Gemma had very similar feet; narrow with a high instep. Gemma was just half a size bigger. But they would do.

Gemma looked up at her friend gratefully. "Thank you," she whispered.

She stripped off her sweat pants and started tying the shoes as quickly as she could. She checked to see if The Banshee was watching. Instead, there on the other side of the studio was Marley, chatting away to The Banshee, clearly distracting her from Gemma's dilemma.

Gemma smiled. What would she do without her amazing friends? She felt her heart calm a little. She took a deep breath as she tucked in her ribbons. She stood up and shook out her legs.

All the time her mind was darting from one thought to the next. What had she done with her shoes? She was so preoccupied with Ethan yesterday that maybe she didn't put them back in her bag, maybe she didn't see them last night ... maybe she pancaked the wrong pair? She joined Dineo at the barre and started stretching. She looked across the studio again and saw Marley on her way back over. Just as she turned to face the front again, Gemma spotted Aimee. She was standing behind Marley, a pair of *pointe* shoes tied together at the ribbons and dangling from one finger. They were Gemma's.

"I don't believe it," Gemma said out loud just as Marley reached her.

Marley and Dineo followed her gaze.

Gemma shook her head. "I should have known it was her."

Mrs Babington clapped her hands again. "Come girls, at the barre please."

Aimee walked past Gemma bumping her shoulder. "This is just the beginning," she whispered.

Gemma felt rattled. Aimee didn't get to her when she teased her, when she bragged about how much money she had or even when she threatened her. But messing with her dancing, that was a step too far.

I have to work harder than most just to stay in the school. I don't need Aimee making that any harder than it already is.

She began her first *plié* exercise, but was irritated and distracted. Gemma knew that was what Aimee wanted. She knew Aimee wanted her to have a bad class and look like an idiot in front of The Banshee.

Not today, Aimee, not today, she thought, pushing the super snob out of her head and focusing on her class.

"I don't understand why you don't just give her what she wants so she'll leave you alone. Leave us alone," Dineo asked as the girls sat around a cafeteria table discussing the latest Aimee incident at lunch.

Aimee had thrown Gemma's shoes out the studio window after the class, and it had taken Gemma and

Marley thirty minutes to try find them, making them both late for English.

"Because then she'll never stop!" Gemma said more forcefully than she meant. "Don't you see, Neo, she is a bully. She always wants her own way, because she's so used to everyone always giving in and letting her have her own way. And if it's not us, she'll pick on someone else and try ruin their lives too. It has to stop. The only way is to stand up to her."

Gemma hated injustice. Whether it was directed at herself, at somebody else, at animals, any living thing, really; she could never stand by and allow it to happen. Her friends knew that, but Aimee had brought out something else in Gemma, something fiercer that wasn't prepared to back down.

"Gems is right, Neo," Marley said gently. "If we give into her now, she'll always walk all over us."

"Besides, I don't have anything to give her," Gemma insisted. "The only reason she's so angry is because of Ethan. From the beginning it's always been about Ethan. The first day he arrives, I have to take him around, not her but me. I didn't ask for that. Then I get paired with Ethan for partnering class and that afternoon, bam," Gemma slammed her hand down hard on the table, "there's the note under our dorm door. Then she's falling all over herself to get him to notice her, he doesn't and bam," she slapped the table again, "she shows up during practice and attacks me. Then yesterday Ethan asks me to the ball and this morning, bam, she takes my shoes. You see? She's jealous, not of what I have or what I can do, but because of Ethan. He's the shiny new toy that the spoilt brat wants, only she can't have it. I can't do anything about that. I can't make him like her."

"I guess you're right. Sorry, I just don't want her to mess up our chances for the production," Dineo said quietly.

"I get that, Neo. But I won't let her, I promise. Besides, you have nothing to worry about, that lead role is yours!" Gemma smiled, nudging Dineo with her shoulder.

"Right, today we are going to start making magic together!" Mr Milano told the dancers in partnering class that afternoon. Gemma felt a little thrill shoot through her body. They'd been practising the core steps in partnering for weeks, and she just couldn't wait to put them all together into the actual *Giselle* routines.

"Today we are going to start learning the routine for the grand *pas de deux* in Act II, where the wili have summoned Giselle from the dead and Albrecht has arrived to lay flowers at her grave," he said.

Gemma could see a glint of excitement in the old teacher's eyes, his Italian accent becoming more pronounced as his passion for the story grew.

"This *pas de deux* between Giselle and Albrecht is very romantic," Mr Milano touched his heart. "They are in an enchanted forest. It is dark, lit only by the silver moon. The wili are ethereal. They glow in the moonlight. In the background we see Giselle's grave. It is sad. But there is love. The young girl is dead and the prince is sorry for how he deceived her. The wilis, the *corps de ballet*, line the sides of the stage while the wili queen, Myrtha, watches on," the ballet master said, moving around the room to indicate their positions.

He divided up the group. "Giselle and Albrecht are centre stage, ladies you're stage left and gentlemen you're stage right. Ladies, follow me." Mr Milano demonstrated the first part of Giselle's routine. "And we go again," he repeated the steps two more times. "Ladies, you work on that so long, please."

Mr Milano joined the boys on the opposite end of the room. "Gentlemen, this is what I want from you," he said, showing the boys their routine.

"At this point, Giselle and Albrecht are dancing by themselves on the stage. They have not come together yet. Giselles, I want to see your broken heart. Here is the man who deceived you, you are sad. Albrecht I want to see your sorrow too. You were a horrible man to our poor Giselle over here," he joked.

Mr Milano walked through the two groups of dancers, checking feet and arm positions and correcting steps.

"Very good. Now Giselle, you are downstage left, Albrecht you are downstage right. You have both just begged the wilis to let Albrecht live and not kill him, but the wilis have denied your pleas," he said raising his hand in the "stop" position and looking away to show how the *corps de ballet* would reject the couple's solemn request.

Albrecht you walk backwards to centre stage, Giselle you *bourrée* to the same point, centre stage. Albrecht you come up behind Giselle, and as she meets this point, gently position your hands underneath her wrists and slowly lift them heavenwards. From here now, you dance together. Giselle you bend forward over your front leg to gather the mist at your feet. Albrecht you follow every movement, your hands stick to Giselle's like glue, you shadow everything precisely. You are sorry, you are asking for her forgiveness, so you support her every step," he explained. "Then," Mr Milano called Dineo out of the line, "we go into the turns we practised." He guided Dineo through a turn *en pointe*, standing behind and gently turning her 360 degrees to face the front again. "This leg," he pointed to Dineo's leg that was in *seconde en l'air*, "curves gently behind Albrecht's body as you turn.

"When you face the front again, you prepare for a series of three short lifts, moving towards the back corner, and then towards the front, downstage left, directly in front of Myrtha." He picked Dineo up just off the ground in three short lifts as the two moved along the imaginary line of wilis towards the front where the evil queen would be standing.

Dineo looked beautiful, Gemma thought. She caught her eye just as she and Mr Milano moved past Gemma's row and gave Dineo a thumbs up. The small smile that fleeted across her face told Gemma she'd seen her encouraging gesture.

"Then we move back to the centre, with small lifts again, and it's here that Giselle finally turns to face Albrecht and look at him for the first time. There's a second where they really see each other, they look into each other's soul, before the wilis pull them apart. This is so important, so important!" Mr Milano said emphatically. "This brings the emotion out, allows the audience to see how these two feel about each other. Okay, so working in your pairs, let's take it from the part where you meet in the centre, and Albrecht stands behind Giselle as she gathers the swirling mist off the forest floor."

The dancers split up into their pairs. Gemma hadn't seen Ethan yet. In a way she was glad, she didn't know what to say to him after yesterday, and didn't know what to expect.

She looked up, he was making his way over to her. She could feel her heart pounding in her rib cage with every breath she took.

He grinned his impish Ethan grin. "Hi!" he said when he reached her.

Gemma smiled back. "Hi," she said, quickly looking away.

"Right. Albrechts, take your places behind our Giselles. Mr Rose," Mr Milano called out to the pianist. "And one and two and …"

As the music started, Gemma was instantly lost in the role. She was Giselle in the misty forest with her lost love. She bent forward and gathered the mist around her feet, as she straightened up she felt Ethan's hands gently meeting hers and raising them upwards. The pounding in her chest got louder. They moved through the rest of the routine. Ethan's hands were on Gemma's hips, turning her, then lifting her. The pounding was so loud now, Gemma was sure Ethan could hear it. Then finally she turned to face him. Ethan's ice-blue eyes pierced hers. A bolt of electricity shot through her body as their hands touched, sizzling its way down her spine to the ground. She stared back at him. They were stuck in the moment: Albrecht and Giselle, Ethan and Gemma.

"... for the first time it was very good," Mr Milano was saying.

His voice broke the spell. Gemma realised she was still *en pointe*, Ethan still holding her hands. She felt so many things. She felt Giselle's sorrow. She felt Giselle's love. She felt her own passion for ballet. And she felt Ethan's intense stare. Her pounding heart was deafening in her ears now. Her legs like jelly.

She came down off *pointe*. She blinked her eyes as if to break the connection between her and Ethan.

"Very nice emotion here you two!" Mr Milano patted Ethan on the shoulder and smiled a big satisfied smile at Gemma. "Good, good," he nodded before strolling over to the next couple.

Gemma looked around. The dancers were either marking out the routines again or waiting for Mr Milano's feedback. Nobody seemed to notice Ethan and Gemma's exchange.

Suddenly Gemma spotted Marley across the room. Her eyes were wide with unspoken questions. Clearly she had seen it. "What the ...?" Marley's eyes asked excitedly.

Gemma shrugged at her friend. She didn't know what to think herself. She liked Ethan as a buddy, someone to joke around with. But since he asked her to the dance yesterday she felt … different. Did she *like* him like him? Her mind jumped to the first time they partnered; her heart had done a weird flip. And the second time, her stomach had lurched. She put it all down to nerves and being worried about not getting all the steps right. But maybe it wasn't nerves? Maybe it was the thought of dancing with him? Her mind leapt between Giselle and Ethan, between ballet and the boy in front of her. Which were her feelings, and which were Giselle's? Her head was a jumbled mess.

"You're a much stronger dancer when you lose yourself in the story, Gemma," Ethan said, ripping Gemma from her thoughts.

She looked up at him. Her heart fluttered up into her throat as he said her name, blocking it so that not even one little word could squeeze past its quivering wings.

She managed a whisper. "Thanks."

Gemma looked away again. Marley was practically jumping out of her skin trying to get Gemma's attention.

Gemma just smiled and rolled her eyes. What else could she do? She couldn't shout across the studio, "Something weird just happened with 'just-my-friend-Ethan' and now I have jelly legs".

Gemma scanned the studio again, her eyes coming to rest on Aimee, who was glaring at her. Gemma didn't know what she'd seen, but from the look on Aimee's face, she had seen enough. Her face was red, her eyes mere slits. If she was in a cartoon, Gemma thought, there would be smoke shooting out the sides of her ears.

Gemma shrugged it off.

Mr Milano was back in the front again.

"Okay, okay," he clapped his hands, quietening the chatter that had been slowly rising around him as he made his way through the pairs of dancers.

I want to take it from the top: first we do Giselle's role in the *pas de deux*, then Albrecht's and then his last part together again. *Capisce*?"

"Yes sir!' the dancers said together.

Gemma focused her attention once more on Giselle. Pushing Ethan and Aimee out of her mind and finding herself in the role of Giselle again brought her back to her dancing. She felt every step, and the emotion connected to it.

She held her focus when Ethan's hands touched hers. A tingling feeling waltzed lightly across her body but she ignored it, allowing only Giselle and the sorrowful notes of Mr Rose's piano to enrapture her.

Gemma used this technique to help her stay focused the rest of the class.

She figured Ethan was doing the same. He only spoke to her about their partnering technique and how they could improve it.

Two hours later she felt shattered: she was tired, her feet were sore and she felt emotionally drained as she juggled Giselle's feelings with her own confused tangle of emotions.

Gemma was relieved when Mr Milano finally brought the class to an end.

She slumped down on the studio floor, exhausted, as

she took off her shoes. She checked her stockinged toes: no blood. Yay!

Marley plopped down next to her. She looked at Gemma and smiled.

"What?" Gemma asked.

"You know what!" her friend teased.

"Know what, what?" Dineo asked, gracefully sliding onto the floor next to Marley.

Marley learnt forward and whispered discreetly, "Ethan and Gems were really getting into their roles today."

Dineo raised an eyebrow. "He's a very good dancer," she said matter of factly. "He has excellent technique."

"He couldn't take his eyes off her," Marley whispered again.

"Always whispering. What, are you planning another late-night escape?" Aimee was standing over the three girls, hands on her hips, red-faced and talking very loudly.

Gemma looked up at Aimee. She held her angry stare for a minute, then looked away, and carried on taking off her shoes. She wasn't going to do this with Aimee. Not now, not in front of all the other students.

But Aimee had other ideas.

"What, didn't you tell anybody else about your midnight rendezvous? Oh, sorry," Aimee clasped her hand over her mouth in fake shock, "I thought everybody knew you two snuck out of your dorm at night while the rest of us were sleeping. Doing things you shouldn't be doing," she raised her voice now so all the students could hear. "And we all know the punishment for breaking school rules, don't we?"

Amber and Naledi sniggered behind Aimee, egging her on.

Gemma could feel eyes on her. Everywhere. All the students had stopped what they were doing. They were staring. Watching Aimee in all her glory.

Gemma felt her anger rising.

"But that's okay, because you two don't belong in this school anyway," Aimee snarled. "You," she pointed at Gemma, "are just not good enough to be here. This is a school for real dancers. And you," she pointed at Marley, "well I don't even know how you got here, but you suck and you're poor and you shouldn't be here either."

Gemma's anger reached boiling point. Picking on her because of Ethan was one thing, but dragging Marley into it was unfair.

She snapped.

"What did you just say?" Gemma shot to her feet, bringing her face close to Aimee's.

"You heard what I said. What are you going to do about it?" Aimee taunted her.

"First," Gemma raised her voice, "I'm going to tell you that you're a stuck-up snob." She could feel her body start to tremble as her rage took hold.

"Next I'm going to tell you that we all deserve to be here. Every single one of us," she pointed to the astonished faces of her classmates that surrounded them.

"We might not be rich, we might not be from famous ballet families, and we might not be the best dancers in the world, but we were good enough to make the cut for this school. Just like you. Which means when it comes to this room," she pointed at the studio behind her, "and that barre," she pointed at the barre along the mirrored wall, "we are just like you. We are dancers. So get off that trip of yours because you are no better than the rest of us here."

Aimee was speechless.

Then Gemma saw her eyes flash with renewed anger.

"You still snuck out. At night. I saw you. That's against the school rules. And you're both going down for it," she pushed Gemma hard with both hands. Gemma stumbled backwards, falling over her ballet bag.

Before Gemma knew it, Ethan was standing between her and Aimee.

"No, they're not," he said calmly to Aimee. "We were with them too," he motioned to himself and Mitch. "We're all going down for it. If you report them, you have to report us too."

Aimee didn't say anything, her eyes switching between Ethan and Gemma who was still on the floor.

Marley helped Gemma up.

Gemma lowered her voice so no one else could hear. "I saw you sneak out too," she said to Aimee quietly. "When we went to watch *Swan Lake* at the Nelson Mandela Theatre. I saw you and Amber coming back to the theatre with your dad's driver."

Aimee drew back in shock. She just stood there, her mouth hanging open.

"We didn't tell Mrs Babington, and weren't planning to," Gemma said.

Aimee stared at her coldly.

Gemma realised they'd just beaten Aimee at her own game.

Aimee knew it too. She looked at the four friends that now stood side-by-side in front of her. Her mood instantly shifted from shock to full-blown fury. She spun around and glared at the bewildered faces of their classmates that surrounded them. "If any of you breathe a word of this to anyone, especially Mrs Babington," she shouted, "I'll have you expelled. Keep your mouths shut!" she exploded, turning and storming out the studio.

Chapter 8

"I think we should just go as witches and wizards, it's the simplest idea and we can all dress in black. That way we can't be easily seen when we slip out, and the hats will hide our hair, so if anybody does see us, it will be difficult to tell exactly who it is?" Mitch said.

It was a beautiful warm spring Saturday afternoon. Gemma, Marley, Mitch and Ethan were sitting in the summerhouse thrashing out the details for their rescue mission. Dineo was sitting quietly on the opposite side, headphones on, lost in YouTube videos of *Giselle* solos on her phone.

Things had been really weird since the Aimee fallout. Students who had never spoken to Gemma before smiled at her in the corridors, the SS avoided all contact with Gemma and her friends, and it felt like an oppressive energy had been lifted from the entire school.

Marley was convinced it was because Gemma had stood up to the person who had not only tormented her, but many other people in the school as well. She'd given all those people a voice, and without having to stoop to Aimee's level and be mean.

"Handled like a true revolutionary Gems. Passive

resistance in action!" Marley had said that night. "And you didn't blab her secret out to the whole studio either!"

Gemma still didn't know where it had all come from: the rage she felt, the words that came out, the way she had behaved, it was as though it all happened to someone else and she was just standing on the sidelines watching.

She didn't feel as unnerved as she should have after her showdown with Aimee. She just felt at peace, like she had finally managed to shake off Aimee's hold. Gemma had regained her power, and she would never ever let anybody put her down again.

Although it was Aimee's horrible comments about Marley that forced Gemma to confront the super snob, Gemma suspected part of her rage towards Aimee that day was because she had hit the nail on the head when she said Gemma didn't belong at SABA. Gemma had never told anybody she sometimes felt that way, but Aimee had said it nonetheless and it had cut like a knife.

"I think that could really work," Ethan agreed with Mitch, bringing Gemma back to the rescue plan that was currently unfolding.

She looked up, Ethan was looking at her.

He grinned that cute-boy Ethan grin.

Things had been really weird with Ethan too. Gemma didn't know how to unravel the mish-mash of emotions she felt. Ethan had covered for her when she'd fallen, he'd helped fend off Aimee, he'd given her good advice about her technique, and he was genuinely a nice, funny guy who she really enjoyed being around. But whenever she caught him looking at her, like now, it felt like her whole world stopped spinning, like everything around her was holding its breath. And then there was the strange electricity when their hands had touched. She shivered.

All she did know was that she didn't want be distracted right now. She'd worked too hard for a solo in *Giselle* to throw it all away because a guy liked her. Okay, not just any guy, Ethan Blake, but still.

She smiled back at Ethan before quickly looking away.

"Okay, let's just do it," Marley said. "We can also hide torches and other stuff we might need under our cloaks. The only thing is, where are we going to get the costumes from? We don't have time to make anything before next Friday night."

"I'll ask my mom." Dineo had joined the circle, unnoticed by the others. "I'll ask her to hire them and send them down for us. It's just easier that way."

"Awesome!" Mitch exclaimed.

"Ah thanks Neo." Gemma beamed at her friend. "So let's just go through everything one more time. Tonight Marley and I will tell Emily that next Friday night she has to meet us in the rose garden. The masked ball starts at 6pm, so we'll sneak out at 8pm, meet her there and then go down to the lake where hopefully we'll find Oliver. Then the two souls can be reunited and SABA will be home to two fewer ghosts."

That night, Gemma and Marley waited until 10pm before they snuck out their dorm. It had been so long since they'd last seen Emily, it almost felt like a dream, like the lonely ballet dancer with the broken heart had never existed at all.

Gemma knew they were going to have to be extra cautious, just in case Aimee was sleeping down the passage with one eye open.

The near-full moon outside had leaked large puddles of silver moonlight onto the floor through all the giant arched windows, making it dead easy for Gemma and Marley to pick their way through the shadows.

They tiptoed down the main passage in their socks, up the stairs at the back of the school towards the old studio.

Both girls suddenly stopped.

They'd heard a noise.

Coming from a room nearby.

Gemma couldn't place the sound.

Human or ghost?

Her heart hammered in her ears.

She strained to hear.

It was footsteps.

But not walking.

Dancing.

Gemma and Marley both exhaled the collective breath they were holding.

It was Emily dancing. She was dancing in a different studio tonight.

The two girls moved silently again until they were outside the studio door. Gemma didn't want to startle Emily.

"Emily!" she whispered through the keyhole. Gemma

didn't know much about ghosts but figured they had extra-sensitive hearing. She hoped Emily would hear her.

The dancing stopped.

Gemma put her hand on the door handle. She slowly pulled it down. The door inched open.

"Emily," she whispered again.

Gemma wasn't taking any chances just in case there was someone hiding in the shadows nearby. She decided not to say their names.

"It's us," she said instead.

She gave Marley a "here goes nothing" look and opened the door.

Emily was standing in the middle of the studio floor, her long white nightgown shimmering in the moonlight that pooled around her feet. Her hands were clasped up to her chest, like she was waiting in great anticipation to see the girls.

"Hello Gemma. Hello Marley," she beamed when she saw them.

Gemma didn't think she'd ever get used to speaking to a ghost.

"Uh hi, Emily," she smiled back, gently closing the door behind Marley.

Marley returned Emily's warm smile. "Hello Emily. How are you?"

"I am very well, thank you for enquiring," Emily said, silently floating over to the girls.

Gemma thought Emily looked different. She looked … happy.

As if reading her mind, Emily suddenly began

gushing about what she had been up to since she last saw them.

"Oh it is so wonderful!" she said. "I have been all over the school." She began spinning around, her arms flying out at her sides. "I have visited so many fantastic places! The ballroom is still my favourite, but oh, I do so love your beautiful big library. There are just so many lovely books in there. At night I prefer it here. But I admit I could not tolerate another night in that other studio, my prison. So now I dance here instead."

Gemma laughed. "Wow, you really have been getting out!"

"Oh yes! And I have seen you and Marley quite a few times. I see Dineo is always dancing, and those young gentlemen you brought with you, Ethan and Mitchell, I have seen them too!"

Marley and Gemma chuckled at Emily's enthusiasm.

"They've all been helping us unravel the mystery behind Oliver's death, and how to free you from the school once and for all," Gemma said.

Emily stopped dancing around at the mention of Oliver's death. He face became serious.

"You have discovered what happened to Oliver?" Emily asked, her brow furrowing.

"Yes we have. We found out that he drowned himself in the lake," Marley said gently.

Emily clutched her chest.

"He could not swim," she whispered, shaking her head.

"We also found out that like you, Oliver can't rest in peace. He has been seen at the lake on the anniversary of his death," Gemma added softly.

Emily quietly processed what the girls had said.

"He is sad too?" Emily asked.

"Yes," Marley nodded. "He is. He doesn't know you are here, feeling the same way."

"We think he can't forgive himself for what he did to you, and that is why he is still stuck here. Before you knew the whole story, you couldn't forgive Oliver for what he had done to you either, which kept you here. His guilt and your anger. We thought maybe, if Oliver had the chance to tell you he was sorry, and you had the chance to tell him you forgive him, the spell that binds you to this place would be broken and you would both be free," Gemma explained.

Emily listened intently, still clutching her heart.

"Yes, I think you are correct, Gemma, I think that is the answer." A faint smile crept across Emily's pale lips.

"You can get out of the building on 31 October, right?" Marley asked.

Emily nodded. "You would like me to go and find Oliver? Oh no please, you cannot leave me, you must help me to find him," she pleaded.

"No, we won't leave you!" Marley reassured her. "We thought we could meet you outside in the rose garden at 8pm. Then we would go with you to find Oliver down by the lake."

Emily nodded again slowly as she considered the plan. "Yes, yes, I think that is a very good plan," she agreed.

"Great!" Gemma said. "Unfortunately we have to go now. The last time we visited you we were seen by someone and they've threatened to get us into trouble with the headmistress."

"Oh no, I am so sorry," Emily said. "Who is this person?"

"Just a girl in our class," Gemma said.

"Go on," Emily prompted.

"Her name is Aimee," Gemma rolled her eyes.

"Oh I know that girl. She is very mean indeed!" Emily said.

"It's okay, we wouldn't have met you if we hadn't come that night. It was totally worth it." Gemma winked.

The girls quietly slipped out the studio, melting into the long shadows that now stretched along the passage floor and up along the walls. Silently, the pair tiptoed back to their dorm.

Gemma scanned the corridor outside their room.

It was deathly still.

The silence hurt her ears.

The plan was Gemma would go first and Marley would wait a while before joining her, just in case they were still under SS surveillance.

Gemma took a deep breath and sprinted for their dorm.

Silently she unlocked the door and slid inside the room.

She put her ear to the door.

The corridor was silent.

After what seemed like an eternity, the door nudged open a notch and Marley slipped in.

"Everything okay?" Gemma asked anxiously.

"Yup, I didn't see anyone out there after you came in. I think we're cool," Marley grinned.

There is only one week to go until we cast for *Giselle*, yes?" Ms Dubois was back at school, and chatting to the girls as they warmed up. "The cast list goes up this Friday."

Soft whoops of delight floated up from the group.

Gemma felt a wave of excitement tinged with fear wash over her. This Friday! The names for the solos would finally be up. Would her name be on the list? She knew this week she had to be the best dancer she could be. She had to show her teachers she was ready for a solo.

Gemma worked extra hard in class, and didn't get anything wrong.

In partnering class she maintained her single-minded focus, ignoring any feelings for Ethan that tried to push through her concentration. And in *Giselle* training, she perfectly executed all the solo pieces they were learning.

After her homework, Gemma headed back to the studio where she trained for two more hours.

Sitting on the studio floor alone that evening, she pulled her toe caps off. Her toes were sore. New blisters had appeared and they were raw and bleeding.

Gemma stared at her feet.

Before, she saw the bloody blisters as a sign that she wasn't good enough to be at SABA because nobody else had blisters.

Looking at them now, she realised that wasn't the case.

Inexperience may have given her blisters before, but today, these came from a different place. These blisters were a sign of hard work. Of determination. And of her unrelenting desire to live her dream.

Gemma was drained, her feet pained and her muscles ached all over. But she was on a high.

She smiled to herself.

This was what it felt like to be a dancer.

The next four days were exactly the same. Gemma ate, drank, slept and lived ballet every waking minute. Every day she felt stronger. Her teachers were noticing it too. Gemma felt it was finally her time to shine.

By Friday afternoon, the students could barely contain themselves. For the past few days, every conversation Gemma had overheard had been punctuated with two words: the list. And every time she heard them, a thrill shot up her spine sending tingling little feelings all over her skin.

A cast list going up was always a big deal, but for the Grade 7 students of the SA Ballet Academy, this cast list was the most important ever.

The students were swarming around the studio's huge double doors, buzzing about who was going to get which role.

Gemma shook her head. "I don't think I can take it anymore. When are they going to put it up?" she asked Dineo and Marley, her right leg bouncing up and down nervously.

The girls were sitting on the bench outside the studio, Gemma in the middle, Dineo to her right and Marley to her left.

Gemma bent forward to look down the corridor over the throng of dancers; still no teachers.

She saw Mitch and Ethan. They were sitting further down the corridor on the opposite side with Zack and Brent. It looked like Mitch was impersonating The Banshee, which had the other three boys in fits of laughter.

Ethan suddenly turned and looked straight at Gemma.

He smiled his impish grin and gave Gemma a thumbs up.

She felt her already queasy stomach somersault. She smiled and gave him a thumbs up back.

Suddenly from behind Ethan she spotted Ms Dubois' head bobbing between the students at the end of the passage.

"Oooooohhhhh, here she comes," she said, grabbing Dineo and Marley's hands and squeezing them tight.

The buzz in the corridor rose loudly as other students spotted the petite teacher pushing her way through the crowd.

She had a single piece of paper in her hands.

A piece of paper that could change the students' lives.

Gemma squeezed her friends' hands again.

The sea of students parted in front of Ms Dubois as she made her way to the noticeboard.

The din was almost unbearable.

Ms Dubois turned to face the group.

"Yes, yes, yes ... Shhhhh," she was saying, trying to calm the overzealous mass. "I know you are all excited!" she said loudly. "Shhh, please, you must shoosh now, please!"

The noise dropped. All eyes were on Ms Dubois and her all-important piece of paper.

She cleared her throat. "I have here the cast list for *Giselle*. You have all been performing so beautifully these last weeks, this was a very difficult decision. You are my babies, I love you all so much!" She smiled warmly at the group. "But there are only a few solos. For these, we have chosen the best. I want to say now congratulations to the soloists. To the other dancers, please keep working hard. Don't give up if your name is not on the list."

And with that she turned and pinned the list up on the noticeboard.

The noise level instantly rose.

Students were shouting, crushing to get to the board.

Gemma, Marley and Dineo jumped up.

They rushed forward.

Fear mixed with excitement in Gemma's stomach.

She looked up at the board.

Her heart fell.

It plummeted.

Down, down, down to her feet.

Her name was not on the list. She hadn't made the cut.

Gemma didn't have a solo.

A tidal wave of despair washed over her.

She read and reread the names.

Giselle: Dineo Nyathi
Prince Albrecht/Loys: Ethan Blake
Hilarion: Charles Crawford-Bradshaw
Willi Queen Myrtha: Aimee Atherton
Princess Bathilde: Marley Moon Fields
Prince of Courland: Percival Wetherby
Berthe (Giselle's mother): Amber Goldstein
Wilfred (Albrecht's squire): Mitchell Petersen

Her eyes scanned the list further down.
There it was.
Gemma James.
On the *corps de ballet* list.
Sadness welled up inside her.
It threatened to wash her away.
Gemma couldn't hold it back any longer.
It engulfed her as it flooded over her body.
Up it rose.
It caught in her throat.
She couldn't breathe.
It stung her eyes.
Tears were waiting in the wings, ready to gush out.
She turned blindly.
She pushed her way through the students.
She saw nothing.
"Gems!" Marley called from somewhere behind her.
"Gems wait!"
She pushed through the people.
"Gemma, are you okay?" Ethan's voice drifted into her

consciousness from somewhere next to her. "Gemma!" he lunged for her.

She pushed more, breaking free of the crush of bodies.

She ran.

She didn't know where she was going.

She just allowed her feet to carry her as far away as possible from the list, from the other dancers, from the school.

She didn't care where.

When she finally stopped, Gemma found herself at the furthest corner of the school, where the manicured lawn unravelled into messy brambles and then into the dark forest beyond.

Her heart was beating hard in her ribcage, like it was trying to break free too.

She turned to face the school.

She saw the beautiful old building she loved so much, the gorgeous rose gardens smiling in the sun, and the purple umbrellas of the jacaranda trees laughing in the breeze.

In that moment, she hated it all.

She hated everything.

The tears she'd been clinging onto like a lifeboat in her ocean of despair finally gave way.

Gemma began to cry.

She sat down, leaning against the tree behind her, and sobbed.

She felt as though her heart was broken in two, the pieces floating out to sea, drifting further and further apart.

She couldn't understand why she hadn't gotten a solo. Her mind skimmed over the last few weeks in studio. She'd done everything right.

She'd worked hard, in every class her steps were perfect. She hadn't messed up in solo training, and in partnering her and Ethan had gotten rousing approvals from Mr Milano day after day.

Ethan.

The thought of him made her cry even harder.

He had landed a solo, and not just any solo, the leading male role.

She had been dancing with the best junior guy all the time and she still hadn't made the cut?

She shook her head.

"I must have looked like an idiot next to him," she whispered to herself. "He won't want to go to the dance with me now, that's for sure."

What a mess, she thought.

Gemma put her head back on the trunk of the tree.

She closed her eyes and cried.

Chapter 9

When it felt like there were no more tears left in her body to cry, and no more ways from which she could examine where she went wrong, Gemma finally opened her eyes.

She had no idea how long she'd been sitting there for, but judging by the soft afternoon glow of the sun that was slowly dancing towards the western horizon, it was somewhere near 4pm.

It would be dinner soon. She knew she had to go back, that she had to face her friends. She took a deep breath and slowly exhaled. Gemma reached into her pocket and found her phone. The students weren't allowed to use their phones until after 6pm at night, but Gemma figured her protected hideaway under the cover of the trees was safe enough.

She opened the call log and clicked the first name on the list: mom.

"Hi sweetie!" her mom answered on the third ring. "Is everything okay, Gems?"

Gemma's mom always knew when something was up, but the fact she was calling from her cell during school hours was a dead giveaway.

"Yes mom, everything's fine. I ... I just wanted to

let you know I didn't get a solo in *Giselle*." Gemma felt her throat close up as she said the words out loud, the words that had been tormenting her all afternoon.

"Oh sweetie I'm sorry! I'm so, so sorry Gems, I know how much that meant to you."

Just hearing her mom acknowledge how important it was to her sent a new flood of tears cascading down her cheeks.

"I just don't understand, mom," she said between sobs. "I worked so hard. Everything was perfect and I didn't even get a small solo. Nothing, just nothing! I'm just not good enough."

"Oh no honey, don't say that! Of course you are. They wouldn't have accepted you otherwise. Your teachers saw something in you the day you auditioned, that's why they asked you to join the school. That something is still there Gems, and it'll show itself when the time is right. And you'll be rewarded for it. Your hard work has not been for nothing, I promise sweetie. You just keep doing your best. You're an absolutely beautiful dancer! It's in your blood. It's what you were born to be."

Gemma let her mom's words sink in.

Her mom always knew exactly what to say to cheer Gemma up.

She exhaled loudly.

"Are you okay, hun?" her mom asked gently.

"Yes ma. Thanks. I'll be fine. I'm just … sad."

"I understand. But it won't always be this way. Everyone has to have a turn in the limelight on the stage; next time it will be yours."

Gemma felt better after the call. She slipped her phone back into her pocket and stood up. Her already sore body ached even more after sitting on the hard ground for so long. She shook out her legs to get the blood flowing again. Her mind drifted to Marley, Dineo, Ethan and Mitch. She didn't know what to say to them when she saw them.

She stepped out of the shadows of the trees and walked towards the school.

It wasn't a minute later when Gemma spotted the group heading towards her. Marley in front, leading the charge, closely followed by Dineo and the boys.

"There you are! We've been looking for you everywhere!" Marley said, sprinting towards Gemma once she was close enough. She threw her arms around Gemma's neck. "Oh Gems! I'm so sorry!" she squeezed her best friend tightly.

Gemma felt the tears rushing up again.

But before they could reach her eyes she felt Dineo's arms around her, and then Mitch's and then Ethan's. They piled on top of the petite dancer, absorbing all her sadness.

They hugged Gemma for ages.

"Uh guys, can't breathe," she said, making a gagging noise.

Marley giggled. "Are you sure, Gems? We can stay like this for a little longer, no problem!"

"Gah! Yes! Sure!" Gemma shouted playfully.

One by one her friends peeled themselves off until they were all standing around her.

"Are you okay?" Dineo asked.

Gemma nodded. "I just needed some time."

Marley put her arm around Gemma's shoulder. "Next time, Gems."

Mitchell punched her softly on the arm. "Come on mate, chin up!" His Australian twang made her laugh.

Ethan looked genuinely sad. "Sorry," he mouthed silently.

Gemma nodded again.

"I know it's not the same, but you did get an understudy role," Marley said gently.

Gemma stared at her friend vacantly.

Marley's eyebrows shot up. "Didn't you see it?" she asked.

Gemma shook her head.

"You're understudying Aimee for the role of Myrtha," Marley said.

Gemma's brain scrambled to make sense of the news. She was understudying a solo? Sure, it was Aimee's solo, but it was still a solo. That meant if anything happened to Aimee …

"So all we need to do is get Aimee out the way and the solo's yours!" Ethan said.

"I could always push her down the stairs," Dineo said darkly.

Gemma burst out laughing. "Neo!"

Dineo shrugged.

"See, it's not all that bad!" Marley offered.

Gemma smiled. "Thanks guys."

"Oh oh oh … guess what?" Marley said flapping her

hands excitedly. "Our costumes for tomorrow night have arrived! Neo's mom just dropped them off!"

"Oh cool!" Gemma said, the thought of costumes, masked balls and late night ghost rescues lifting her mood.

"Come on! Let's go!" Marley said, grabbing Gemma and Dineo's hands and tugging them in the direction of the school, with Ethan and Mitchell tagging behind.

Saturday morning dawned bright and sunny. Gemma felt a thousand times better: tonight was Halloween, the masked ball and the night they would finally reunite Emily and Oliver. A thrill of excitement shot through her.

The school was usually quiet on a Saturday, but today it was bustling with activity. The students had been given the day off from dancing and were milling around the campus, laughing, joking and chilling out in the gardens. The Grand Ballroom was being transformed into a haunted house, while lawnmowers buzzed around the gardens like busy worker bees preparing the grounds for the ball.

Gemma was lying on her stomach on the lawn outside the summerhouse, her legs crossed in the air behind her, watching two weaver birds build their nests in a nearby tree.

Marley was leaning against Gemma, trying to stick a pair of black feathers onto her mask.

Dineo sat crossed-legged opposite Gemma, thoroughly engrossed in a ballet magazine her father had posted to her from China.

Gemma took in the scene around her: teachers yelling instructions, the maintenance crew scurrying around with clippers in their hands, students frantically finalising their costumes for the ball. She smiled. She just knew it was going to be a good day.

"Oh no!" Marley wailed.

"What's wrong?" Gemma asked over her shoulder.

"I messed up my feathers. The glue has stuck all the fluffy bits together! Now I need to go get some more! Arghhh!"

"I was going to go to the bathroom. I'll get you some on my way back," Gemma offered.

"Aw thanks Gems!"

Gemma jumped up and made her way to the bathroom. She crossed the lawns and headed for the big stone stairs that connected the two wings of the campus.

"Uh, Gemma?" she heard a voice behind her say when she was halfway up the stairs.

She'd recognise that voice anywhere. Her heart quickened. She turned to see Ethan standing a few steps below her. His hands were thrust deep into the pockets of his faded jeans, his head tilted to one side as he regarded her, ice-blue eyes looking almost supernatural in the sun.

She felt a delicate flutter of wings in her stomach. "Hey Ethan," she said calmly as she turned to face him. He was coming to tell her he couldn't take her to the ball anymore, she knew it. She didn't blame him. After all, the best male junior dancer in the school wouldn't want to be seen with someone from the *corps de ballet*, of that she was sure.

"I just wanted to say that you didn't get a solo not because you don't dance well, but just because some of the other girls were better. This time. Next time will be different. I've seen from my mom's career, ballet can be fickle. Don't stop trying; you're a brilliant dancer," he said earnestly.

"Thanks Ethan. That means a lot coming from you."

He climbed up the stairs between them until he was at her eye level. "About tonight …"

Here we go, she thought, sucking in her breath.

"I just wanted to see if you're still cool to go with me?"

She blinked. What? He still wanted her as his date for the ball? Why?

"Gemma?"

"Uh, yes."

"You don't sound so sure. You don't have to if you don't want to?"

"No. I mean no, that's not it, I do want to. I just didn't think you'd still want to go with me?"

He held her gaze. "Of course I still want to go with you."

Gemma instantly had jelly legs again. "Uh, okay, good, yes, right, I'll see you tonight then," she nodded. "Gotta go," she mumbled as she backed up the last remaining stairs before turning and sprinting for the bathroom.

"Good, yes, right …" What was that? Gemma always felt so in control of everything but when Ethan was around, it was like she suddenly got a bad case of stage fright. Like the music was playing but she'd forgotten all the steps. She shook her head; she felt like she was going crazy.

It was 5pm, there was just one hour to go until the ball began. Gemma and Marley were in the dorm putting on their costumes.

Gemma couldn't wait for the evening to start.

It was obvious the other students felt the same way too: from beyond the dorm door the girls could hear people shrieking and running down the corridors. Music was blaring from the matric dorm block and over all the noise, the booming sound of a voice over a microphone could be heard repeating "testing, testing 1,2,3" coming from the Grand Ballroom.

"What do you think?" Marley held up her hands. Long black fake nails stuck out the ends of a pair of black elbow-length gloves that she'd cut off at the fingertips. "Witchy enough?"

"Yes!" Gemma laughed. "I think your idea of a wig was a better one. Straightening this mop is going to take all night," she moaned, trying to tame her thick wavy hair with a straightening iron.

Marley had shoved her blonde curls under a short bob-length wig of straight black hair. She'd paired this with a long, flowing strappy black dress that hung in layers to the ground and her self-made long black cut-off gloves.

Gemma had chosen a long black dress that floated just above the floor and hugged her lithe ballet dancer body. It had long tatty bell sleeves that danced in the air when she moved her arms.

"That will just have to do," Gemma said, running her fingers through her now dead straight hair that fell down to the middle of her back. "And now for the fun part!" she said, holding up her stage makeup bag.

"Yipeee," said Marley, who'd been waiting all week to put on her ghoulish witch face.

Gemma leaned up close to the mirror. She concentrated as she pulled a thick black kohl liner under her eyelashes.

"Do you think it'll be easy reuniting Emily and Oliver?" she asked Marley, bringing the liner out past the corner of her eye, Cleopatra style.

Marley patted a makeup sponge laden with pancake across her cheeks, smothering her freckles. "I think so. I mean, we just need to get to Emily and then hope Oliver appears like Mr Rose said he would. The hardest part," she raised both eyebrows cheekily, "is not getting caught."

"I know. I hope Ethan's plan works and Zack and Brent create enough of a distraction so we can get out. And back in again," Gemma said, tracing a similar shape underneath her other eye. She did the same on the top of her eyelids, before standing back to admire her handiwork.

She turned to face Marley. "How does this look?"

"Oh cool! It's so goth!"

"Perfect!" Gemma smiled. "Now for the finishing touch," she said, puckering her lips up to the mirror and dabbing black lipstick on them.

"That looks so rad!"

"Thanks, Marls, you want black lips too?"

"Nah, I'm going for blood red, to match my cape!"

As a surprise, Dineo's mom had hired each of the girls black velvet hooded capes. Marley's was lined with devilish red satin and Gemma's with vampy deep plum-coloured satin. Ever the ballet dancer, Dineo's cape was lined in soft ballet pink satin.

Gemma put her cape on and tied it around her neck. She popped the hood up over her head and looked in the mirror. Good, she thought, mysterious enough to fit the part and dark enough to get lost in the night when they slipped out the ballroom later.

She helped Marley put on her cloak. With her mischievous smile, Marley reminded Gemma of a naughty Red Riding Hood on her way to fight the big bad wolf instead of falling prey to his pranks.

"Oh, we almost forgot, our masks!" Marley said.

She had chosen a simple black mask that just covered her eyes, and had embellished it with the most gorgeous black feathers that conjured up images of the black swan from *Swan Lake*.

Gemma had gone for a traditional Venetian masquerade mask in delicate black filigree that had cats' eye-shaped holes for the eyes that curled up into two points above her eyebrows. The middle came down into a small point that rested just above the tip of her nose.

"Oh my word, Gems, you look beautiful!" Marley said once the mask was on.

"Thanks Marls, so do you!"

Just then the grand old school tower clock boomed. It was 6pm.

"Hooooo," Gemma said excitedly, "it's time, it's time!"

Gemma pulled her hood over her head.

Marley did the same.

"Right. Deep breaths!" Marley instructed. "Do you have your torch?"

"Check!"

"And your phone?"

"Check!"

"Then we're good to go!" Marley declared.

Gemma and Marley stepped outside Fonteyn House; the scene before them took Gemma's breath away.

All the old stone paths leading to the Grand Ballroom had been lined with strings of fairy lights. Their bright yellow glow burned holes in the night like fireflies at play.

The Grand Ballroom had been superbly dressed for the ball; swathes of white chiffon had been draped in flowing crescent shapes across the outside walls, and old black wrought iron lanterns with giant white candles inside lined the stone stairs leading up to the giant arched wooden front doors that boasted oversized garlands of vines spray painted silver and entwined with toy black snakes.

Toy bats in various sizes floated up from either wreath over the front of the two doors and across the ballroom wall.

Soft yellow light spilled out of the tall arched windows on the front and sides of the building, making it seem taller, grander and more imposing.

Gemma was mesmerised.

The school looked completely different. It was as

though Cinderella's fairy godmother had waved her wand and transformed the school into a magical fairyland, with the Grand Ballroom its enchanted castle.

Gemma squeezed Marley's hand. "Wow! Look at the ballroom!"

"I know!" Marley whispered excitedly.

Jovial groups of cackling students disguised as witches and wizards, fairies and phantoms, and goblins and ghouls danced down the fairy paths towards the hall, sweeping up the girls along with them.

Gemma pointed to the front door. "Look, there's Neo!"

Marley waved wildly at her friend to get her attention.

With her simple long black dress, pink-lined black cape and soft pink and black satin mask with silver glitter detail, Dineo looked more dark princess than wicked witch.

Dineo spotted them. She gave a little wave as she walked across the landing to the balcony.

Gemma laughed; Dineo really was like a princess, she thought, complete with a royal wave.

The girls bounded up the stairs towards their friend.

"You look gorgeous, Neo!" Gemma said.

"Oh yes!" Marley agreed. "Not ghoulish at all, just plain beautiful!"

"Thanks guys, you both look amazing. I love the makeup!"

"Well, shall we?" Marley asked, offering an arm to each girl.

Somebody cleared their throat behind the girls.

"Ahem, I do believe that's our job?"

Gemma spun around to see two very well disguised wizards standing behind them. If Ethan hadn't spoken, Gemma would never have recognised him. Or Mitch, for that matter.

Their heavy black robes hung to the floor. Long black hair stuck out of two pointy wizard hats, and was matched in front by two incredibly long black beards. Just their eyes were visible, over which they'd placed simple black eye masks.

Gemma tried hard not to laugh.

They looked like two apparitions clad from head to toe in black.

She felt Marley's body begin to shake next to her. Her friend was stifling her laughter too.

"What?" Ethan shrugged.

"You can call us The Dark Lords," Mitch said in a low gravelly voice.

Gemma couldn't hold it in any longer and collapsed on top of Marley in a bout of belly laughs.

Marley clutched her friend and laughed too.

"What?" Ethan asked again, his face dead pan. "You told us to," he dropped his voice, "blend into the dark."

Marley got her giggles under control. "It's just that you're both so … so well disguised! There isn't an inch of the real you visible anywhere!"

Mitch stepped up to Marley and grabbed her hand and dropped down onto one knee. "Ah but mademoiselle, my lips, they are still visible," he closed his eyes and puckered his lips up to Marley.

All three girls were now struck by uncontrollable laughter.

Ethan laughed under his breath, shaking his head.

Mitch still had his lips pushed out in a big pout. "So, how about it, beautiful?" he asked, batting his eyelashes at Marley.

Marley leaned forward and offered Mitch a perfectly pancaked cheek.

Mitch made a loud kissing sound as he planted a big kiss there.

Ethan rolled his eyes playfully at Gemma.

"Come on, Casanova, let's escort the ladies in," Ethan said, heaving Mitch up off the floor.

Just then Luc Delacroix, a French exchange student in Grade 9, appeared behind the guys.

"Dineo?" he asked.

Everyone turned to look at the soft-spoken Frenchman who was known to be one of the academy's best dancers.

Gemma shot her friend a "what-aren't-you-telling-us?" look.

Dineo ignored her. "Hello, Luc," she said politely.

Marley stuck out her hand. "Hi Luc. Nice to meet you." She grinned.

"Ah, sorry, these are my friends – Marley, Gemma, Mitchell and Ethan. This is Luc."

"Hi Luc," Gemma smiled.

"Hello, hello, hello," he said, nodding at each one. "Nice to meet all of you."

The enormous wooden doors to the Grand Ballroom suddenly swung open.

144

The Banshee stepped out, dressed as what appeared to be a ghost, in a white sheet with gaping misshapen holes over the eyes. She fumbled with the sheet, trying to see through the openings.

"Listen up, listen up!" she shouted across the sea of students that took up the entire landing, the stone staircase and part of the garden below. "You will please enter the Grand Ballroom in an orderly fashion, like this," she motioned to the masked head girl, Summer Bailey, and head boy, Bryce Jamieson, who were standing on the landing next to her.

Bryce lifted his hand towards Summer, and turned his palm upwards. Summer gently placed her hand in his and the two strode into the ballroom.

"Such pomp and ceremony!" Gemma whispered to Marley.

"I'll have no shouting and no pushing, please. I now declare the South African Ballet Academy's first masked ball open!" The Banshee said with a sweep of her ghostly hand towards the doors.

Gemma, Marley and Dineo took their places alongside Ethan, Mitch and Luc in the queue of students.

Gemma slid the hood of her cape off her head, revealing the full beauty of her costume and mask, which was framed by her glossy straight raven hair.

She turned to look at Ethan.

From behind his mask Gemma saw Ethan's eyebrows shoot skywards.

He didn't say anything. He just held her gaze, smiled at her and offered his hand.

Gemma dropped her eyes to the ground shyly as she rested her hand in his.

She turned to face the doors and stared straight ahead.

She could feel Ethan still staring at her as they waited in the line.

Then it was their turn.

Gemma stepped across the threshold; it was like stepping into another world.

Gigantic crystal chandeliers hung on long chains from the high roof, the same soft white chiffon had been draped along the walls carrying strings of fairy lights that twinkled from within their delicate folds.

Over this old world ballroom glamour the teachers had added a subtle layer of Halloween horror.

Silver cobwebs hung from the arched windows, spiders dangled from the chandeliers and rows of old crooked graves peered out from the top of the stage, watched over by a large silver moon that had been suspended from the ceiling low over the stage.

Tall black coffins stood in the four corners of the room, their doors open to reveal skeletons arranged in different poses as they attempted to "climb out" of their eerie caskets.

And in the middle was the dance floor, where a group of students was doing a zombie dance to the music blaring from the enormous speakers on the sides of the stage.

It was the ultimate Halloween ball, Gemma thought. "Wow! This place looks amazing!"

"I know! It's like old and cool and scary all at the same time!" said Marley.

Gemma spotted the SS standing to one side of the dance floor. They were all there; Aimee, Amber, Naledi, Percy, Charles and another masked boy Gemma didn't recognise.

Instead of ghosts and ghouls, Aimee had dressed as the queen she believed she was, flanked by her two princesses, Amber and Naledi.

Their Marie Antoinette-style dresses were big and pouffy and ornate.

All three girls had their hair up in dramatic up-styles, Aimee with a large crown perched right on top.

The guys wore leggings and long coats in hunter green and ruby red, embellished with gold brocade. Shoulder-length white wigs curled up the sides of their faces making them look like old court judges.

"Arghh … she just couldn't help herself, could she?" Marley asked.

"There's an upside to it." Gemma grinned cheekily. "They'll never be able to follow us in that getup! I'm sure you can see those enormous dresses from the moon!"

Ethan suddenly pointed to the other side of the room, to two wizards who were dressed exactly the same as him. "There's Zack and Brent."

He whistled a strange whistle that cut through the music.

The two boys turned in unison to look at Ethan before winding their way through the people to where Gemma, Ethan, Marley and Mitch were standing.

They too were so well disguised, Gemma couldn't tell

which boy was which.

"Looking good, Blakey," one of the boys said to Ethan, punching him playfully on the arm.

Ethan laughed. "So do you!"

"Hi," the two boys said together to the rest of the group.

"Zack," Ethan said, motioning to the one on the left, "and Brent," he said pointing to the other.

"Thanks for helping us out tonight," Gemma said.

"No problem, we owed Ethan one," Zack said.

"Love the costumes, although I think I've seen them before?" Marley giggled.

"Just a little decoy to throw the SS off our scent," Ethan grinned from behind his black wizard beard.

Mitch stepped forward and lowered his voice. "Let's go through the plan one more time. At 7:45 you two are going to go to the main doors to create a distraction. We sneak out behind you, do our thing, and call you on your phone when we need to get back in?"

"Yup," Zack said.

Gemma thought carefully about the plan. "What's the distraction?"

Brent stuck his hand inside his wizard coat and produced a large white rat with bright pink eyes.

"This is Bear, our pet rat," he said.

"Oh cool! You keep him here, at the academy?" Marley asked, wide eyed.

"Yup, we have a big cage in our room that we just cover during inspection. Had him for two years now," he said proudly.

"And Bear's going to help us by …?" Gemma asked,

unsure of the rat's exact role.

"Bear loves running up our arms and sitting on our heads. He has great balance and can stay there even if you shake your head around. It's his favourite thing to do. So we'll show him to whoever is on door duty and as soon as he spots their arm, he'll take off for their head!" Brent explained.

"While Brent pretends to try catch Bear, I'll duck behind and open the door for you," Zack said.

"And then we'll spread open our capes like a black wall in front of the door and you can slip out, unnoticed," Brent finished.

Gemma had been listening intently. "Sounds great. What about getting back in?"

The two boys exchanged doubtful looks with one another.

Zack wrinkled his nose. "Ummm, we haven't quite figured that out yet."

"We know we can't pull the same stunt the second time around so …"

Marley shrugged. "We could just wing it? Call you guys when we're outside the door?"

"I think we should do that," Ethan agreed.

A loud piercing screech ripped through the hall.

Students covered their ears.

"Hellooo, hellooo." The Banshee was on the stage tapping the microphone violently with her finger.

The sound system screeched again sending up a collective groan from the students on the dance floor below.

"Ahem," she cleared her throat.

"Distinguished guests, teachers, learn–" she broke off, suddenly realising she was still in her white sheet. She tried to pull the sheet off with one hand, microphone in the other hand. She got tangled in the microphone cable and began flapping around.

"Whooooohoooooo," one student trilled from the back of the hall, sounding just like a ghost in a scary movie, sending a wave of laughter up from the students.

The Banshee fumbled and flapped, the sheet billowing out about her.

"She looks like Emily on a bad day!" Gemma whispered to Marley who turned her face into her cape to stifle a laugh.

The sheet finally gave up the fight.

The Banshee managed to tug it off her head and threw it onto the ground indignantly.

Hair standing on end, glasses skew on her nose, Gemma thought the headmistress looked terrifying just as she was!

"Ahem …" She cleared her throat into the microphone again.

"Distinguished guests, teachers, learners, thank you all for joining us tonight on the occasion of our first ever masked ball. It's fitting that we gather here in this room tonight, for this was once the Grand Ballroom of Forestlake Estate – the site of many wonderful balls among the lords and ladies of Johannesburg who were the benefactors of this great school …"

The Banshee droned on for what seemed to Gemma

like forever, talking about the history of the school, the early ballets that were performed at the school and the difficulties it faced during World War II.

Gemma's stomach clenched into a knot when The Banshee reflected on the Smythe family and how the school was originally built to further the dreams and aspirations of a dancer just like them – Emily Smythe.

She wondered about Emily waiting for them outside in the rose garden, about reuniting her with her long lost love and about finally setting her free from the school – a place she had once loved so much but that in the end had become her prison.

She thought about Oliver and what it would be like to see him, having learnt so much about him these past months.

What happened if he rejected Emily – what would they do then?

Would Emily freak out and turn on them?

No, Gemma didn't believe that would happen. She believed in true love; she believed Oliver would die for Emily all over again if it meant she would forgive him for marrying Lily.

Gemma realised just how much she'd become involved in Emily's story, and the significance of saying goodbye to that sad, lonely dancer she'd stumbled upon just a few months ago.

She would miss Emily.

She liked the fact that she and her friends had a secret that nobody else in the school knew about. A secret as cool as the school's resident ghost. And that they managed to figure out the mystery surrounding her death.

Releasing Emily from the school once and for all would close that book forever.

Loud clapping and whistling from the students wrenched Gemma from her contemplations.

"Cool, next Friday off, awesome!" Marley shouted above the applause.

Gemma quickly hid her confusion. "Uh, totally!"

The Banshee was tapping the microphone loudly again. "Food will be served now, please help yourself to drinks and snacks. And then enjoy the ball!"

The students clapped loudly as the DJ turned up the music.

"Oh, and unmasking will take place at 11pm!" The Banshee shouted over the music, which gradually drowned her out.

"Can we get you ladies something to eat and drink?" Ethan offered. "May as well eat now while we can?"

Gemma nodded. "Good idea. What's the time?"

Ethan checked his watch. "7:15. We've got thirty minutes."

"Cool, you guys get drinks, we'll get food?"

Mitch and Ethan headed off to the drinks table.

"Luc and I are going to stand over there," Dineo pointed to where Luc's friends were. "I can see the whole room from there. I'll call you on your phone if I see anything you need to know about."

Gemma smiled. That was Dineo's way of saying, "I've got your back". She knew her friend cared for them and didn't want to see them get into trouble, even if she never said so.

Gemma leaned over and gave Dineo a big kiss on her cheek. "Thank you."

Dineo nodded, and then she and Luc were gone, swallowed up by the dancing horde of scary masked beings.

Marley nudged Gemma. "Now, about that food …"

"Are you hungry again?"

"Always!" Marley laughed, tugging Gemma off to the food table.

The girls piled their plates high with sarmies, samoosas, sausage rolls and little meatballs speared onto toothpicks with slivers of gherkin.

"My, we do have a large appetite," Aimee said, seeing the two overstuffed plates as the girls left the table.

"Not as large as that big pouffy meringue you're wearing," Gemma said, staring straight ahead and pushing past Queen Aimee.

The boys were already there, waiting with glasses of juice.

"Mmmm, yummy!" Mitch said, spotting the teetering plates of food. "I'm ravenous!"

They divided up the food and scoffed it down.

"Everyone ready?" Ethan asked. "It's time."

Gemma felt her body tense with excitement. She exhaled loudly. "Right." She downed the last of her juice and popped up her cape hood. "Let's do this thing!"

Marley, Mitch and Ethan followed suit.

They slunk along the wall, inching closer to the big double entrance doors.

Gemma in front, Marley behind, followed by Mitch and Ethan.

They saw Zack and Brent approach the doors.

Ms Dubois was on duty with Ms Shaw, the librarian.

Two women and a rat. This should be interesting, Gemma thought.

She led the group slowly down the wall.

Zack produced Bear from inside his cape.

Gemma was just half a metre away now.

Gemma spotted Bear leap out of Zack's hands and take off up Ms Dubois' arm.

The ballet teacher screamed.

Ms Shaw turned to help her.

Bear leapt from Ms Dubois' head to Ms Shaw's head.

Ms Shaw shrieked and batted at her head where Bear was now perched.

Ms Dubois used a clipboard to try swat the rat off the librarian's head but was too short and couldn't reach.

The music drowned out their yells and squawks.

Gemma glanced around the room quickly.

No one was watching the spectacle.

She pulled her cape around her body, her hood down low.

Brent lunged for the door and pushed it open.

Quick as a flash he opened his cape.

Zack did the same, shielding Gemma from the teachers.

She sucked in her breath.

Dashed forward.

And slipped out the door.

As soon as she was out she raced down the stairs and hid behind the landing's balustrade in the garden.

She waited for three more figures to do the same.

Just metres from the ballroom door, and covered only by some thin bushes, she surveyed the garden.

The moon was full.

Typical, she thought, a full moon on Halloween.

The perfect scene setter? Yes. Handy when you're trying to undertake a covert operation at night? Not so much.

"We'll have to keep to the shadows. The moon's too bright," she whispered over her shoulder.

"Let's stick to those trees to the right, and then the right balustrade down those stairs, and then go round the back of the summerhouse. Cool?"

"Yup," said Marley.

"Cool," the boys whispered in unison.

Gemma darted from shadow to shadow, like a dragonfly flitting between lily pads, constantly scanning the grounds in the silvery moonlight for the slightest movement.

Finally they were at the summerhouse.

Gemma slipped behind the old building.

She exhaled sharply.

So far, so good, she thought.

Marley and the boys slid around the corner next to Gemma just as the school's old tower clock chimed eight.

"Good timing," Marley winked at her friend.

Gemma nodded. "Now let's go find our ghost!" she whispered.

From the summerhouse it was a short walk to the rose garden, which was filled with hundreds of roses of virtually every colour.

The cream and white flowers glowed under the full moon.

And it was from this bank of almost ghostly blooms that Emily emerged.

"Oh, my! What a curious outfit you have on Gemma! Oh my goodness, all of you!" she said floating forward towards the group.

"Hello, Emily." Gemma smiled warmly. "It's finally the night, when you get to see Oliver again."

"I am most grateful for all your help. I have truly longed for this," Emily said earnestly.

"It's been our pleasure!" Marley said.

"We were happy to help!" Ethan added.

"Okay, we need to get to the lake, but we can't cut across the lawns, it's too risky. So we have to go the long way around, sticking to the tree line," Gemma whispered. "It's going to take a while, so let's go."

The group walked in silence. Ethan and Mitch hung back after a while to make sure they weren't being followed, Marley stayed upfront with Gemma and Emily.

"How can I ever repay you for all you have done?" Emily eventually asked.

"You don't have to repay us! You needed help and we were able to help you. Simple as that," Gemma said softly.

"Yes, but you did not have to. I will find a way to show you my appreciation, I promise you."

"If you insist." Gemma smiled again.

Just ahead Gemma could see how the edge of the lawn gave way to mossy forest floor, dark and gloomy, the dense canopy of leaves shielding much of the moonlight.

The perfect line of trees they were walking along was soon a tangle of bramble bush. The group fought their way through the bushes that were now bathed in deep shadows while Emily hovered nearby.

"I can see a footpath up ahead, Gemma," Emily suddenly said, motioning to the right of where they were currently battling the wild undergrowth.

"Thanks!" Gemma said gratefully, struggling to untangle her cape from the grip of a particularly stubborn branch.

Emily waited at the path.

Marley was first out of the scrubby bush and headed over to Emily, followed closely by Mitch.

"You okay?" Ethan asked Gemma.

She laughed softly. "Yes, it would be great if I could just. Stop. Getting. Tangled!"

Ethan strode through the bush to Gemma and helped untangle her cape.

She bent forward to show Ethan where she was caught.

Ethan leaned in to get a better look, and they bashed heads.

"Aw!" Gemma yelped.

"Oh no, sorry!" Ethan said.

Emily let out a little giggle. "They are very sweet together, are they not?" she asked Marley.

Marley giggled too. "Oh yes they are!" she agreed.

Gemma was still rubbing her forehead when Ethan freed her from the brambles.

Marley and Mitch led the charge now along the winding forest path, their ghostly friend to whom they would soon bid farewell wafting alongside.

The trees grew together much closer now. It was cooler. The air smelt damp and earthy, and the ground was a silvery patchwork of dappled moonlight, fallen leaves and deep green moss.

Gemma realised they were in the heart of the forest now.

Ethan shot her an apologetic sideward glance. "Sorry again about your head."

"It's okay. Marley would say there wasn't much in there to start with!" Gemma joked.

An unexpected opening in the canopy above allowed a luminous moonbeam to cut through the murky forest.

With her hood on and the soft silvery light playing across her face, Gemma looked like a magical being herself.

"You look very nice tonight," Ethan said coyly.

What, was that a little shyness from the usually confident Ethan Blake? Gemma wondered, smiling to herself.

"Thank you, Ethan."

The forest closed in around them again and they walked in silence behind the others.

Gemma suddenly thought she heard music.

"Shhh," she whispered softly to get the others' attention.

They all stopped.

"I think I hear music."

The others strained to listen.

"It is music, Gemma, you are right. I can hear, it is coming from over there." Emily pointed to what looked like a clearing in the forest, behind a bank of tall, thick-trunked trees.

The group fell into single-file behind Mitch who'd offered to go first.

Emily hung back at Gemma's side.

They crept slowly through the shadows, the music getting louder.

It reminded Gemma of the music from the second act of *Giselle*, when Albrecht goes to Giselle's grave. It was sad and forlorn.

Mitch stopped at a large tree that had fallen across the path.

He bucked down on his haunches.

Gemma, Marley and Ethan quickly joined him.

Slowly, they lifted their faces to peer over the trunk.

The scene before Gemma was like something she had only ever dreamed about.

It was picture perfect, like a ballet set.

The lake stretched out before them in a tranquil glade, radiant and shimmering in the light of the moon.

It was framed by enormous, ancient trees that were dark with shadows and embellished with vines that hung low down to the ground.

And in the centre of the lake, drifting just above the water and moving in glorious swirls and twirls like mist in the morning, was a troupe of ghostly dancers.

Gemma blinked.

She looked again.

They were still there.

The forlorn music was actually their eerie wails.

Their bodies moved in time to every supernatural note, rising, falling, cloaked in silver mist, and with pitiful faces filled with grief.

Her heart caught; were these wilis? Like in *Giselle*? Would they try claim Emily as one of their own? Even worse, what would happen when they discovered there were humans in their midst?

She looked quickly at Marley.

Her friend was totally hypnotised: eyes wide, focused on the mesmerising scene in front of her.

"What if they're wilis?" she whispered as quietly as she could.

Marley's face suddenly fell.

She turned slowly to look at Gemma, her face fixed in a grimace.

"Oh crap," she mouthed silently.

"These spirits are not wilis," Emily whispered. "They are water nymphs. They dance to console those who die of a broken heart. They are dancing for …"

Emily stopped abruptly.

Gemma turned back to the lake.

There walking along the shore towards them was Oliver.

She guessed he was about 18 when he died.

Dressed in a pair of pants rolled up at the ankles and secured on the top with braces, his ghostly form cut a lonely figure as he traced the water's edge. Hands in his pockets, staring blankly at the moon above.

Emily was rapt.

She watched Oliver.

Every step he took.

Oliver sat down on the shore, hugging his knees to his chest.

He put his head down on his forearm.

"You have to go to him," Gemma whispered to Emily.

Emily couldn't drag her eyes away from Oliver.

"I'm scared," she said softly.

"He loved you, Emily. He will want to see you again," Marley reassured.

Emily hesitated.

Eyes still fixed on Oliver, she rose above the tree trunk they hid behind, and sunk down the other side onto the sand.

Immediately the nymphs stopped wailing and dancing.

The glade fell silent.

Oliver looked up across the lake.

The nymphs hovered above the water, faces turned towards Emily.

Slowly, Oliver turned his gaze to where Emily was standing.

Gemma could clearly see his face. Subtle changes in his expression, his energy, his body, told the story of the emotions he was feeling.

Shock.

Disbelief.

Realisation.

Oliver slowly stood up.

His whisper was barely audible. "Emily?"

Emily was still floating just in front of Gemma and the group.

She nodded silently.

"Emily?" he said again, louder.

Relief.

Joy.

Love.

Oliver's essence seemed to suddenly glow brighter.

He moved swiftly across the shore.

Emily did too.

They met in the middle, stopping just a breath away from each other.

Gemma couldn't see Emily's face, but Oliver's look was hopeful. She knew exactly what he was hoping for: forgiveness.

Emily was talking. Gemma couldn't hear what she was saying.

Then Oliver was talking. He was shaking his head. He clutched his chest. Tears streamed down his cheeks.

Emily was nodding.

Oliver stepped forward and gently kissed Emily on the forehead.

That was it, Gemma thought. That was the moment they'd been waiting for. Emily had forgiven Oliver, and he had forgiven her.

The nymphs had been silently watching from their watery stage.

Now instead of desperate wails, their voices united in a song of happiness.

The spirits began to move again, twisting and turning to the melody.

Oliver took Emily's hand and they danced along the shore.

For the first time, Gemma saw Emily's face.

Gone was the lost and lonely spirit they had found, and in her place was a delighted soul, blazing brightly with happiness.

For the first time in a hundred years, Emily was dancing with a heart filled with love, not anger.

Gemma watched as she leapt and twirled across the sand.

The couple floated across the water, joining the nymphs in an intricate whirling dance.

Gemma marvelled at how effortlessly their bodies flowed to the rising and falling singing.

She leaned into Marley. "They're all absolutely beautiful to watch, aren't they?"

Marley nodded.

More than just light and airy, Gemma could feel the real emotion in their dance. She could sense the renewed adoration between Emily and Oliver, and the amazing support of the water nymphs who had clearly been Oliver's only company for the past century. Now they danced out of love too. These feelings were palpable to

Gemma, and left a lump in her throat.

"They dance with their heart," Marley said. "They don't worry about the steps, they just go where the music takes them."

Gemma watched; Marley was right.

The spirits didn't listen to the singing, trying to match their steps to it. They just felt the music. And their bodies simply drifted along to it.

Faintly, in the distance, the school tower clock chimed nine.

Marley nudged Gemma. "We better go."

Gemma didn't want to leave the fairy tale scene.

She also wanted to say goodbye to Emily, but there was no way to get her attention.

She'd thought so much about Emily over the past few weeks, and they'd put so much effort into her rescue, it felt wrong to just leave.

And there was so much she wanted to ask her.

How could they possibly just go and not say goodbye?

They'd never see her again.

Gemma felt sad, and agitated.

"Gemma, we have to go," Ethan said firmly.

She turned, the others were already back on the path waiting for her.

She looked back at the lake.

Why hadn't Emily said goodbye?

Tears stung the backs of her eyes.

"I'm coming," she snapped at him, more harshly than she meant to.

She followed him onto the path, and gave a final

glance over her shoulder. Emily and Oliver were gone.

With a heavy heart she trekked back with her friends through the forest.

Once out of earshot, Mitch and Marley started chatting excitedly about what had just happened. Mitch imitated the nymphs and Marley laughed.

"Are you all right?" Ethan asked.

"I'm fine," Gemma said bluntly, still irritated that he'd pushed her to leave.

"She's just a ghost," Ethan shrugged, "it's not like she was your best friend or anything."

Irritation flashed through her.

"You wouldn't understand."

"I just think it's no big deal. She needed rescuing, we rescued her, now we need to get back or we'll be the ones needing rescuing."

"It was a big deal to me. This was our thing, me and Marley and Dineo. I didn't ask you to be part of this, you wanted to be."

"Yes but …"

Gemma stomped past Ethan to catch up with Marley and Mitch.

Mitch got the hint and hung back to wait for Ethan.

Gemma didn't know why she was so irritated. Ethan was right, Emily was just a ghost. What was the big deal?

She told Marley about the spat, and her friend put an arm around her shoulders as they walked.

It wasn't long before they were at the edge of the forest, the lawn stretching out before them towards the Grand Ballroom.

Gemma went ahead and retraced her earlier steps. Around the outskirts of the lawns, along the tree line, back through the rose garden, around the back of the summerhouse, from tree to tree around the lawn and to the bushy garden next to the ballroom stairs.

She didn't want to talk to Ethan, so motioned for Marley to tell him to text Zack and Brent.

After a minute, he gave them the thumbs up.

The group silently left their hiding place.

They climbed up the stairs towards the big entrance doors.

And walked slap bang into The Banshee.

Chapter 10

Gemma's heart froze.

She couldn't believe it.

They'd been so careful.

"And where are you lot coming from, hmmm?"

The group said nothing.

"Who have we here? Unmask yourselves, now!"

They silently removed their masks.

"Ms James, Ms Fields, I expect nothing less from the two of you. But Mr Blake … I am disappointed."

The Banshee glared at them, silently taking in each dancer. Her beady eyes came to rest on Gemma, and drifted down to a clump of brambles that had gone unnoticed, clinging to a corner of her cloak.

"Do you mind telling me exactly where you lot have been?"

"Ah there you are my dearies, I wondered what had happened to you," Mr Rose said as he came shuffling up the stairs towards them.

He got to the top of the stairs and leaned on the balustrade while he caught his breath.

"You have something to say, Mr Rose?" The Banshee asked, irritated with the sudden turn of events.

"Yes, yes, Mrs Babington, I've been looking for these four dearies. You know," he dabbed his face with his handkerchief, "my memory is just not as good as it once was. Just this morning I couldn't find my shoes! Can you believe it, my shoes! Ha ha ha," he chuckled.

Mrs Babington was not amused.

"Well, get on with it! Where have they been?"

"With me, of course, in the music room. I asked them to help me find a special piece of music I had planned for the unmasking ceremony later. It's ever so spooky and so dramatic. Very Phantom of the Opera!"

The Banshee stared at him blankly, like the old man had truly lost his marbles.

"They were helping me look for the, for the ... now what do you call that thing again ...?"

"The CD, Mr Rose," Ethan offered helpfully.

"Yes, that's it! Well done, old chap!"

"Did you forget that you sent us back here to the ball when we couldn't find it anywhere in your music room?" Gemma prompted gently.

"Yes my dearie, that's right, I sent you back here. I remember now," he smiled a triumphant smile at Mrs Babington.

"Hmpfff." The Banshee snorted disparagingly. "Mr Rose, I have no idea what you are talking about, and these students know better than to break the school rules."

"We just wanted to help Mr Rose with the surprise he'd planned for you, ma'am, we didn't mean to get into trouble," Mitch said with the biggest, saddest puppy dog eyes he could muster.

The Banshee had a huge soft spot for Mitch.

She exhaled loudly and shook her head.

"Very well. But next time, Mr Rose, please follow protocol and get permission first! Now inside, all of you!" she boomed as she opened the ballroom door.

The group walked past Mr Rose as they filed into the ballroom, each giving him a silent thanks as they did so.

The old man just nodded at them, a smile playing at his lips and a mischievous twinkle in his eye.

Gemma couldn't shake the feeling that Mr Rose knew more about Oliver than he had let on when they had spoken to him.

She was sitting on the side of the ballroom staring vacantly into space, her mind retracing every detail of the evening.

Marley and Mitch were dancing, and Dineo was still hanging out with Luc somewhere in the crowded room that throbbed with booming music.

Around her people danced and laughed and whooped with delight.

She felt the exact opposite: sad and alone.

Gemma hadn't seen Ethan since they'd come back; Zack and Brent were waiting at the door as soon as they walked in, and wanted to know every detail of the Great Bust and subsequent Great Save by Mr Rose.

Ethan had been regaling them with all the juicy bits ever since, she imagined.

Or maybe he just didn't want to be anywhere near

her after she snapped at him.

She still felt angry at him.

Was she being unfair? Didn't Ethan know how much Emily meant to her?

Gemma thought about that. Why did Emily mean so much to her?

Then it hit her. She was just like Emily.

They both loved to dance.

They both wanted more than anything to shine on the prestigious Academy stage.

And they had both been denied that chance.

Gemma realised her sadness wasn't only about missing Emily now that she was gone, but having to let go of the idea that there was no longer someone in that old school building who was just like her.

Emily had found her happily ever after.

Would Gemma ever have that too?

She was so lost in her thoughts, she didn't even notice Mitch standing in front of her.

"Hey girlfriend, whazzup?" Mitch shouted above the music.

She looked up at him, a deep frown across her brow as she tried to gather her thoughts.

"Oh, hi Mitch! Nothing … sorry, was just thinking about stuff. I'm good!"

"Then come on, up you get," he said, hoisting Gemma from her chair. "You're coming with me!"

Mitch marched Gemma over to the circle where Marley was waiting for her.

Dineo and Luc were there too.

Marley gave her friend a huge hug as she joined the circle. "Nice of you to join us," she teased.

Gemma nudged her playfully, and soon they were all dancing to the music.

At 10:59:50 exactly, a countdown begun.

"Ten … nine … eight … seven," the students shouted together, "three … two … one!"

As they reached "one" and the old tower clock struck 11pm, a massive cheer went up from the dance floor and they all threw their masks up into the air.

Gemma spent most of Sunday getting everything ready for school and rehearsals the next day.

Marley had volunteered to help clean up the ballroom after last night's dance, so Gemma had the dorm all to herself.

She used the time to pancake her *pointe* shoes – the ones that Aimee had stolen, reattach a ribbon to a shoe from the other pair, and check all her homework was done. While carefully stitching the loose ribbon back onto her shoe, Ethan floated into her mind.

She thought again about everything that had happened last night.

How Ethan said it was time to go after Emily and Oliver danced off together, and how she had snapped at him.

He couldn't possibly have known why I felt so sad about Emily. I only just figured that out myself. And he was just trying to help, to make sure we didn't get into trouble. I'm such an idiot!

Gemma's mind flitted to Emily.

She knew Emily was grateful for their help. Gemma realised Emily had just been too caught up in the moment of seeing Oliver again to say goodbye.

If it had been me, I'd probably have done the same thing.

For the first time, she understood Emily hadn't meant to not say goodbye. It just happened.

So, as Marley would say, it was time to put on her big girl panties, suck it up and get on with life.

"Besides," her friend reminded her that night while chomping on a mouthful of mac and cheese, "there's something else that needs your attention now. Like a little upcoming production and your role as an understudy."

"Finally, some sense." Dineo looked heavenwards like she was thanking the gods.

"Hey!" Marley said in mock disgust, hands on her hips.

Gemma had been pushing *Giselle* out of her mind, mostly because she couldn't bear the thought of having to work with Aimee, which she was going to have to do every day for the next four weeks starting tomorrow.

"Seriously, the next month is going to be hectic. We have *Giselle* and finals coming up, so I think a little less of all this stuff," Dineo waved her hand around vaguely in the air, "and a little more of what we came here to do."

Gemma could see Marley felt as told off by Dineo as she did.

"Okay, I promise, no more funny business," Marley said, holding up her right hand in a scout's promise.

Dineo shot her a sarcastic look.

Marley giggled.

"We promise, Neo, no more ghosts, just ballet," Gemma clarified.

Dineo folded her arms. "And no more boys either," she declared.

"Oh right, says the girl who has clearly won the heart of one of our best dancers?" Marley teased.

The embarrassed look that crept across Dineo's face told Gemma that Marley was onto something.

She wondered if Dineo's declaration wasn't more for herself than for Gemma and Marley. Gemma knew the last thing Dineo would want now would be the distraction of a certain brilliant French dancer.

"Well, Ethan isn't speaking to me anyway, so you don't have to worry about me there," she said, poking at her pasta with her fork.

Gemma didn't feel like getting into the Ethan thing, so she changed the subject. "I can't believe it's just four weeks till curtain up. And I can't believe I have to work with Aimee. Of all people."

"Focus," Dineo said simply.

Gemma looked up at her.

"Never forget why you're here; why you do what you do every day. Focus on that, not on Aimee."

The next morning started with a bang, as Gemma found herself in Studio D at 8am sharp standing behind Aimee, learning the steps to Queen Myrtha's solo.

Gemma was relieved to see Ms Dubois was taking the class, and that she was already waiting for the girls when they arrived. There was no time for Aimee to say anything to Gemma, which suited her just fine.

That didn't stop Aimee from giving Gemma the occasional high and mighty Queen Aimee look. Just to make sure Gemma knew she was the understudy.

"After Hilarion has come to visit Giselle's grave, it is Myrtha who arrives in the glade first, yes?" Ms Dubois explained. "Sensing her there, Hilarion flees the forest. Myrtha performs this solo in the graveyard, alone. It is, how you say, little scary, there is just the graves, the forest and the silent moon. The dance is sombre. Also, not forget, Myrtha is fearsome, she is wicked. It is also powerful, strong, showing the spirit queen's strength."

It was quite an easy solo, Gemma thought. It was slow and controlled in the beginning, but changed midway. She loved the *Grand battements* at the end that led into a series of *chaînés* turns on the diagonal. The movements mirrored the tempo of the music. As the music climbed, the wili queen spiralled faster, and faster, and faster across the stage towards the audience, ending on the final note right before them.

"At this point," Ms Dubois motioned to the sides of the studio, where the wings on the stage would be, "Myrtha summons the wilis from their graves – the *corps de ballet*. And Giselle appears on the stage for the first time since her death. She is a wili too now, yes? She dances with Myrtha, here in the front of the stage. The *corps de ballet*, all the wilis, is behind you now. The two dancers loop through the wilis in a figure of eight, la la la la ..." Ms Dubois traced the direction Myrtha would take, "and then you end up here. And that is when our dear Prince Albrecht enters the scene, heartbroken, and lost in the forest, looking for Giselle's grave."

Ms Dubois then took the girls through the steps, over and over they repeated the series of slow *arabesques*, the *Grand battement* and *pirouette* combinations, and the intense *développés en pointe*.

Gemma could feel her body start to ache, her feet especially.

After four hours, she was grateful Ms Dubois called it a day.

Gemma deliberately hung back after class to ask Ms Dubois on which days she would do her *corps de ballet* training so she wouldn't have to be alone with Aimee.

The rest of the week was the same: Gemma found herself running between Studio D on a Monday, Wednesday and Friday for four hours of Myrtha training, and Studio B on a Tuesday, Thursday and Friday afternoon for another four hours of *corps de ballet* training. And every spare second in between, she studied for final exams.

The next two weeks were the same.

Ballet, ballet, ballet, study, sleep. Repeat.

She hadn't seen Ethan for three weeks, although she'd heard he had blown Mr Milano away in training.

She caught up with Dineo and Marley over hasty meals in the cafeteria, and of course chatted to Marley at night, but even that was rushed, as Marley usually got back to the dorm late from training, just before Gemma fell asleep.

The only highlight was trying on their costumes.

The wilis wore beautiful dresses of soft white tulle, with simple sweetheart necklines and thin straps.

Myrtha's dress was similar, just with a slight silver leaf detail down the front of the dress that the seamstress said she would add on should Gemma need to step in for Aimee.

Gemma knew that wasn't going to happen, but humoured the wardrobe manager anyway.

The last week of November, the week before the production opened, was crazy.

There were dress rehearsals every day, in studio and in the theatre, for both productions: the Grade 7s' *Giselle* and the Grade 12s' *The Nutcracker*.

It was early on a Monday morning. The first rays of dawn hadn't even pricked the summer sky yet. But Gemma couldn't sleep.

Her blistered feet pained, her muscles ached all over and she was worried about the next three weeks that lay ahead. Would she manage to fit everything in – her studies for finals and rehearsing?

She tossed in her bed.

She knew everyone faced the same challenge, but rushing between the two training sessions was starting to take its toll on her.

While other students were recovering from the day before's training, she was in her second session.

What happened if she forgot the *corps de ballet* steps? Or got them mixed up with the Myrtha solo? What happened if her toenails fell off again? The one was lifting, she was sure of it.

Irritated, Gemma got up.

Whenever she felt wound up like this, she would dance. It was the last thing she wanted to do, but she felt she needed to be at the barre, to be doing something to take her mind off the thoughts that were running circles in her head.

She slipped on a pair of tights and her favourite leotard, throwing on a pair of sweats and a hoodie for the walk from the dorms to the studio.

She grabbed her ballet bag, and after checking on a gently snoring Marley, tiptoed out the door.

Gemma warmed up at the barre, going through the same movements she had been doing every day for the past 10 years of her life.

Her body was on autopilot, her mind thinking back to the last month. So much had changed. She'd never worked harder in her whole life. She'd hardly spent time with her friends. And she hadn't seen Ethan at all. Emily was gone. And Halloween night seemed like a weird dream, like it had never happened at all.

Gemma propped her leg up on the barre and slid down the length of it, stretching her legs. She dropped her forehead down onto her knee. She liked the pull in her hamstrings. It was a comforting pain. She stayed like that for ages.

"Never forget why you're here; why you do what you do every day. Focus on that." Dineo's words rang loud in her ears.

She might have offered the advice for dealing with Aimee, but Gemma realised they were words of wisdom she needed now.

Why was she here? Because she loved to dance. But then why did it feel so difficult? Surely if it's something you love so much, it should come easily? It did for Marley, for Dineo, and even for Aimee. Dancing came easily to them. Why did Gemma always feel like she had to work double as hard to achieve the same results as them? And even then, she thought, her mind running through the millions of dances she'd seen her friends perform over the years, they looked different on stage. Effortless. Flowing. Melting. Just like the water nymphs had.

What had Marley said? Oh yes, "they dance with their heart. They don't worry about the steps, they just go where the music takes them."

That's how Gemma used to dance. That was when ballet was still fun for her, when she didn't worry about every little step and if she was doing it perfectly right. That was when she danced for the love of dancing, nothing else.

She propped her other leg on the barre and slid down, dropping her forehead onto her knee.

Gemma knew all the steps for the Myrtha solo. What happened if she just forgot about her feet for now, and let them do what they knew they needed to do? What happened if she shifted her focus away from her feet, and into her heart? She was supposed to be dancing like a spirit. And she was fortunate enough to have really seen spirits dance. So she knew how they moved.

She had seen how they dipped and flowed and totally surrendered to their haunting song.

She moved to the centre of the studio. She took out her phone – Dineo had made sure they all had the music for their solos and the *corps de ballet* on their phones so they could practice. She thumbed through the music in the menu until she found Myrtha's solo. The music boomed loud in her ears. She shoved the phone into the top of her leotard, and closed her eyes.

She let the music wash over her.

She pictured Hilarion on the stage, saying his goodbyes to Giselle's grave.

The music boomed again, indicating the wilis were nearby.

The music reverberated through Gemma's body.

Hilarion continued his sorrowful farewells.

The music boomed again, highlighting Myrtha's presence on the stage.

The music seized Gemma, somewhere deep down inside.

The music climbed as the fearful Hilarion took off.

Gemma felt her body starting to mirror the flow of the music.

There was a lull in the score.

And then the daintiest little notes as Myrtha *bourréed* onto the stage.

Eyes still closed, Gemma *bourréed* across the studio floor. She forgot about her feet completely, turned off her brain, and allowed her body to feel the music.

As the tempo quickened, Gemma's body raced ahead.

As the music slowed, Gemma's body did too.

She was completely one with the music, there was no separation between the sound she felt inside her body and the way her body responded to it.

She gave in to the *pirouettes*, spinning dizzyingly across the room; she felt every inch of the *arabesques*, right to the last second, before she flowed into the next movement; and she let the music lift her leaps to heavenly heights.

She was weightless, ethereal, surreal.

She completed the last step and finished the piece, her arms floating out at her sides, and her head tilted slightly backwards.

Her chest heaved up and down.

She had completely surrendered to the music.

That was what she was born to do. That was why she here.

Gemma inhaled deeply to catch her breath, and opened her eyes.

She heard muted clapping behind her, and realised her headphones were still in. She pulled them out and spun around. It was Ms Dubois, and she was beaming.

"Oooh la la la, Gemma!" she cried rushing over from the door where she had been watching. "I haven't seen you dance like that since you first come to the academy!" She caught both Gemma's hands in hers. "That, my dear, that is dancing. You were beautiful! No, exquisite! Why you not dance like that for Ms Dubois before, hmmm?"

Gemma was overwhelmed and embarrassed all at the same time. "I ... I ..."

"You felt the music. You forgot the feet, yes? Yes! Ballet is technical, but the good dancer doesn't dance with the head, the good dancer dances with the heart. Today, you dance with the heart. Today, Gemma, you are a ballerina!"

Gemma flushed with happiness as Ms Dubois wrapped her arms around her and squeezed tight.

"Gemma, you dance like that next year, and a solo will be yours. No more understudy for Gemma, yes?"

Gemma's body shook with a combination of absolute elation and pure adrenaline.

Mwah! Mwah! Ms Dubois kissed Gemma on each cheek. "Now, you keep dancing like that!" she shouted as she headed back to the door where she had dropped her bags when she came in.

Gemma shook her head. That's what had been missing. She'd been too caught up in the technical detail of what she was doing. Now she saw why her teachers were always telling her to soften her body, to relax her face, to give in to the movement a little more. She never understood that. But now she did. She got it. And it made perfect sense.

That afternoon they did their first run through of the production in theatre, in costume, from the top with all the dancers.

Gemma was super excited to watch Dineo and Marley. She'd only heard bits about their solos, and couldn't wait to see them dance.

Gemma was only in the *corps de ballet*, but after this

morning, she was totally okay with that. She was going to be the best damn wili anybody had ever laid eyes on!

When she got to the dressing room, her costume was already hanging at her dressing station, courtesy of Marley who was hopping around in excitement.

Gemma caught Marley's shoulders, pulling her friend down and rooting her to the spot where she stood. "Calm down, you're going to hurt yourself!"

Marley fanned her face with her hands. "I know, I'm just so ... oooohhh," she trilled as she spotted Dineo at the dressing room door and ran over to usher her in.

Marley had made sure the three friends had three dressing stations in a row. It was an unspoken law, wherever you sat for the dress rehearsals was where you sat during the production.

Each dressing station had hooks on the walls for the costumes, a mirror with lights all the way around, a little vanity for putting your makeup bag on, and a chair.

Gemma hugged Dineo. "Hey stranger!" she said.

"I know! I could say the same about you!" Dineo said as she hugged Gemma back.

"This is sooo exciting!" Marley enthused, jumping from one foot to the other.

"I think you need to stop hopping around like a crazy thing and get dressed," Gemma said.

Speakers on the wall played the music that was currently playing on stage so you could hear when it was near your turn to go through to the green room.

"This is the first call for the peasants, Giselle, Hilarion, Wilfred, Albrecht, Berthe," the speaker crackled.

"Ooohhh," Marley said again, rushing over to put her costume on. "Help me with this zip, Gems?"

Gemma laughed under her breath and pulled up Marley's zip.

Although she wasn't needed on stage until the second act, Gemma wanted to watch Dineo. And Ethan. She'd been thinking a lot about him and their fight, and she wanted to say sorry. She hoped to get a chance after the rehearsal was over.

She zipped up Dineo's costume and helped her put her headdress on: a simple garland of flowers that Giselle wears in her hair in the opening scene.

"Enjoy it, guys!" she said to them once they were ready.

Gemma was left in the dressing room with the other *corps de ballet* dancers. She put on her tights and shoes, so all she'd have to do was slip into her dress a few minutes before. She pulled on her sweats, and padded quietly out the dressing room, through the green room and backstage. She knew she had to keep out of everybody's way, especially the technicians who worked the lights and music; they could get really snippy with the dancers.

The first act had just opened, and the village peasants were doing a traditional folk dance.

Dineo was gorgeous, of course. Every step neat, and just the right amount of poise and emotion.

And then she saw Ethan. She could see why Mr Milano had been so impressed: Ethan was faultless. His technical ability, the way he moved and the expression on his face, you would swear he really was Prince Albrecht and he really was in love with Giselle. Everything about him was just perfect.

Gemma remembered how it had felt dancing with him; his hands so strong, so sure on her waist. She moved closer to the stage in the wings, and watched the two of them dance. Neither dancer saw her, but she admired them the entire time, completely in awe.

Gemma never got a chance to talk to Ethan that day, or the rest of the week. The days were long and crazy with rehearsals every day at the theatre, and then cramming for exams at night.

That weekend all the students had to stay at the school; there were no outing privileges because of the exams.

Gemma and Marley were swatting in the library; Dineo and Ethan were in studio ironing out some issue with one of the lifts.

Marley yawned loudly. "Can't we take a break?" she whispered to Gemma.

Gemma pulled a face. "Yes, please, this stuff is so boring," she said, pushing her books away.

The girls escaped into the sunshine, and picked a spot on the lawn to laze for a bit. Gemma loved the feeling of the soft, spongy grass under her back and the bright summer sun on her face. She was so exhausted, she let her eyelids close softly.

Marley was droning on in the background about something, but Gemma's overstuffed mind refused to listen. She mumbled "hmm" in what seemed like appropriate places as Marley carried on.

Suddenly all Gemma's sun was blocked out. She tugged one eye open sleepily to see who the culprit was. It was Ethan.

She quickly pulled herself upright, blinking as the bright sunlight flooded over her. Her head was still stuck in dreamland.

"Sorry, didn't mean to wake you," he joked. "We're done in the studio."

Gemma looked around. Marley had Mitch engrossed in the story that had put her to sleep, and Dineo was sitting next to Gemma, head in her ballet bag, looking furiously for something.

"Oops," she said sheepishly, scratching her head. "Marley's story was a little … uh, involved." She grinned.

"I heard that!" Marley shot back from behind her.

Gemma ignored her and stood up. "I actually wanted to talk to you," she said to Ethan. She walked away from the group and Ethan followed.

"I … I … I just wanted to say I was sorry. For shouting at you in the forest. I didn't mean to. I was just …"

Ethan was biting his bottom lip. He didn't say anything.

Oh no, he's really angry with me.

"… disappointed. With Emily." She looked down at the ground. "And I took it out on you. And that was stupid."

Ethan was still silent.

She looked up.

185

He was still biting his lip.

"Say something?"

Ethan's lips widened into a huge Ethan grin.

"Nah, it's cool, I just wanted to see you squirm," he laughed.

"What? I'm like dying over here and you're like …" she swung at him with a fist that connected him on the arm.

"Aw!" he cried, still laughing. "Sorry!"

"Ethan Blake, you're going to pay for that!"

"No seriously, I'm sorry," he stopped laughing. "And I'm sorry about Halloween too. I spoke to Marley and she told me how much Emily meant to you. I didn't realise that. I shouldn't have said she was just a ghost. I thought you were really angry with me, so I've kind of been keeping a low profile."

"Me too. I mean, I thought you were mad at me, so … same."

"Friends?" he asked holding out his hand.

"Friends!" Gemma smiled, shaking it.

"Sold out! For the next two weeks. Every night is sold out!" Dineo was standing in the doorway of Gemma and Marley's room, a rare smile on her face and a glint of excitement in her eyes.

"Wow! That's amazing. Imagine all those people who are going to be watching your every move, every night, Neo. No pressure!" Marley joked.

Dineo sucked in a breath. "I know, right?"

For the first time ever, Gemma thought she saw

just a hint of nervousness dance across Dineo's usually composed face.

"You'll be fine, Neo. You know every step, you and Ethan have got all your *pas de deux* stuff right, and you look absolutely beautiful on stage. You are the best Giselle the Academy has ever seen!" Gemma reassured.

Dineo titled her head to one side. "Thanks, Gems."

In just three hours, the school would lift the curtain on its most anticipated ballet production ever: a double bill of *Giselle* and *The Nutcracker*, involving all the school's pupils, from Grade 1 to matric.

Gemma's stomach was a jumble of excitement and nervousness and happiness all rolled into one.

Dineo exhaled loudly, "I need to go get ready. I'll see you guys in the dressing room?"

"Yup," Gemma and Marley nodded together.

"I'm really happy for Neo," Gemma said after she was gone. "She really deserves this. She has worked so hard for it."

"Totally," Marley agreed. "But the next two weeks are going to be tough. On all of us."

"I know. I think this must be what it feels like to dance for a company. Every day, ballet, ballet, ballet. It's all you do. In the studio, on the stage, in the studio again. It's hectic, but it's worth it. Imagine just dancing all day. No school, no homework!" Gemma laughed.

"No Banshee waiting around every corner," Marley waddled across the room, pointing her finger accusingly at Gemma as she looked over the top of non-existent glasses that were invisibly perched on the tip of her nose.

"Ha ha ha." Gemma threw her head back as she laughed.

It felt good to be silly with her best friend again. The last few weeks had been difficult and confusing. But now she had sorted out her feelings over Emily, cleared up things with Ethan, and rediscovered her love for ballet. All she wanted to do now was get on that stage and dance!

"Come on." She launched a pillow at Marley's head. "Let's go get ready."

As Gemma and Marley walked along the corridors, streams of excited junior grade children swept past them. They were being corralled from the sides and the back by stressed out teachers who begged them to walk and not run in the corridors, and packs of moms who were buried under piles of tulle and satin.

"You sound like baby elephants!" a teacher shouted somewhere down the corridor. "Walk like the ballet dancers you are supposed to be!"

Gemma laughed. It sounded just like what Mrs. Siyankovsky used to say to Gemma and Marley when they first came to the academy.

Dineo was already in the dressing room, and was focusing intently on unpacking all her makeup onto the vanity.

Gemma and Marley dumped their stuff next to her.

"Hey Neo!" Gemma said.

"Hi," she waved vaguely with the other hand, not

looking up as she continued to unpack her makeup.

Almost every older dancer in the academy had a ritual they did before going on stage, and beware the person who dared interrupt them.

Dineo's pre-stage ritual was to make sure everything was in the exact same place as the first time she had danced in a major production. That was when she was just five years old, and had danced the role of Clara in *The Nutcracker* at the State Theatre in Pretoria.

Since then, every time she went on stage, she did the same thing: unpacked her makeup onto the vanity in the same order; checked her costume, tights and shoes; stretched; did her makeup; stretched; put on her tights, shoes and a leotard; warmed up her feet *en pointe*; put on her costume; had someone check her costume three times to make sure everything was in place; and then sat quietly to run through her various dances in her head. She never spoke to anyone, and remained entirely focused on whichever part of the ritual she was busy with. And she took it all very seriously.

Gemma and Marley knew this, so got on with unpacking their stuff.

Marley chatted constantly about nothing in particular.

"Oops, sorry," someone said next to Gemma as her wili costume landed on the floor. She knew instantly who it was, and that that wasn't a real apology.

Gemma turned, her makeup sponges still in her hand.

It was Aimee, holding up her Myrtha costume that had mysteriously knocked Gemma's costume off its hook.

"Sorry, I didn't see your little dress there over this big costume I have for my role as Myrtha," Aimee declared, her fake apology soaked in sarcasm.

Amber and Naledi cackled behind their costumes.

"That's okay, Aimee," Gemma said smiling sweetly, "we all know your head is stuck so far up your butt, we're amazed that you can see anything at all."

All along the row of vanity mirrors girls burst out laughing, even some of the Grade 12 girls.

Aimee glared at Gemma before stomping off.

Marley nudged her. "Nice one, Gems!"

Gemma took her time doing her makeup, applying a light pancake base to her face and blending it down her neck, across her collarbones and along her shoulders. Next she added dramatic eye shadow, bold eyeliner and a set of fake eyelashes.

"This is your one-hour curtain call, one hour curtain call," the dressing room speaker boomed.

Gemma checked the clock. She'd wanted to grab a chocolate earlier – her only pre-stage ritual, if you could call it that – but hadn't had a chance.

"I'm just going to the vending machine quick, do you guys want anything?"

"No, I'm cool, thanks Gems," Marley answered from under the vanity where she was trying in vain to untangle the cord to her hairdryer.

Dineo's steely stare told Gemma she was zoned out and hadn't even heard her.

She ran out the door and into the passage that

separated the boys' and girls' dressing rooms. Right at the end was the vending machine. She sprinted towards it.

Just at that moment the toilet door opened. Before she could stop, Gemma crashed into the person who'd just stepped out.

She went one way, he went the other, and they both landed on their bums with a rather loud thud.

She looked up, startled, blinking her eyes with their enormously long fake lashes.

Her eyes ran over the ensemble before her: a pair of guy's leather ballet boots, leggings and a tunic fit for a prince.

Her eyes met his.

Ethan.

"I'm so sorry." She burst out laughing. "I didn't even see you there!"

He stood up, rubbing his backside. "I'm not surprised, you were going so fast!" he laughed.

Ethan held out his hand and hauled Gemma up off the floor.

"Geesh, The Banshee would have me for supper if I damaged her star performer an hour before curtain up!" Gemma winced.

Ethan chuckled. "I'm cool. You?"

Gemma scrunched up her face as she rubbed her butt. "Cool," she said.

"Where were you going in such a rush?"

Gemma could feel her cheeks heat up as she jerked her thumb over her right shoulder to the vending machine behind her. "Chocolate."

Ethan laughed. "Oh, right! Sure you're okay?"

Gemma nodded. "Yup. Thanks. I gotta go!"

"Of course. Don't let me stand in the way of a girl and her chocolate!" he said sweeping his arm towards the vending machine.

Heat tickled Gemma's cheeks again. "Thanks!"

She walked the rest of the way, aware of Ethan lingering in the corridor behind her. By the time she'd gotten her chocolate and turned back, the passage was empty.

She raced back to the dressing room, which was humming with activity. Makeup was going on, girls were slapping La Pebra's onto their hair, and there were periodic flurries of tulle and satin as costumes flashed past.

Marley was wrestling with the hairdryer, trying to tame her curls.

"Need some help?" Gemma offered.

"It's just hopeless!" Marley wailed.

With much coaxing, and tons of La Pebra's, Gemma managed to get Marley's hair to behave.

"Oh, what would I do without you, Gems?" Marley cried, rushing around looking for her ballet bag.

Gemma laughed as she settled down and twisted her own wavy hair into a bun, pinning it down. A lick of La Pebra's here and there, and her hair was done. She did her makeup, leaving her lips for later.

"This is your thirty-minute curtain call, thirty-minute curtain call," the dressing room speaker declared loudly.

"That's just enough time to eat this," Gemma said,

leaning back in her chair with her chocolate in hand, "and put on my costume."

Marley was still faffing with her makeup. "Please remind me to start earlier with all this stuff tomorrow night," she said, as she dragged the mascara brush across her lashes with a shaky hand.

"You've got time. I'll help you with your dress as soon as you're done."

Gemma munched away at her chocolate silently while the rest of the dressing room battled misplaced shoes, uncooperative costumes, and laddered tights. The nervous excitement in the air was laced with the smell of hairspray, a dozen different types of deodorant and rosin, which floated up from the box at the door where the dancers dipped their shoes on their way out.

Dineo was dressed and ready for the stage. "I'll see you guys out there. Break a leg," she whispered as she headed off to the green room.

Gemma helped Marley put on her Princess Bathilde costume.

"There, you're look perfect!" she said admiring the finished look.

There was just 15 minutes to go. All the lead performers were due back stage now.

Gemma's phone beeped.

Break a leg (not your butt) tonight. E

It was from Ethan. Gemma laughed out loud.

Get your butt backstage before The Banshee kicks it for you

Lol. OK cool. Later

193

Gemma didn't even know Ethan had her number. A ball of warm fuzziness bounced around in her tummy.

"What are you smiling at?" Marley asked, eyeing the phone in Gemma's hand.

"A text I just got."

"Oh cool. Your mom?"

"Uh no. From Ethan."

"And?"

"Just saying break a leg."

"Just saying break a leg? There's nothing *just* about that! He's supposed to be backstage already! He could get into big trouble for texting you now!"

"Marley Moon Fields, to the green room please," Mrs Johnson, the Grade 2 teacher, called from the dressing room door.

Gemma gave Marley a quick hug. "Break a leg!"

"And you, Gems!"

Marley disappeared through the door.

The room was much quieter. Only the *corps* dancers were left, and the Grade 12 girls.

Gemma checked her makeup again, and puckered up her lips as she added a touch of dark red lipstick with a small brush. She blotted her lips on a piece of tissue, reapplied the colour and blotted again.

She balanced the headpiece on her head, a delicate garland of snow white flowers, and clipped it into place.

She put on her shoes, being careful to tuck in the ribbons. She moved to the warm-up barre and stretched, her mind running through the steps she was about to perform.

The dressing room speaker suddenly leapt to life, as the first strains of the first act of *Giselle* blared through it.

It was time for the part Gemma loved the most – putting on her costume.

She carefully stepped into the fairy tale white dress with its soft layers of fine tulle that fell to just before the floor. At the back, in the small of the back, it had two small, dainty wings.

Gemma reached her hand behind and pulled up the zip. The finishing touch was a soft tulle veil that all the wilis wore over their heads and that hung down to their waist. Under the stage lights, the veils accentuated the wilis' ghostly appearance.

Gemma looked in the mirror. She held her breath. She looked like a real ballerina.

Mrs Johnston returned with her clipboard. "*Corps de ballet* to the green room, please."

Gemma was waiting in the wings. That familiar feeling of nervousness twisted in her stomach. She hoped she wouldn't forget the steps, and prayed she wouldn't make any mistakes.

The scene before her was dark and eerie. Soft blue light bathed the stage, mimicking the glow of a full moon. The forest stage set of tall trees surrounding the glade cast dark shadows across the stage. In the far corner was Giselle's grave. Charles was there, on one knee, dressed as Hilarion, lingering at the gravesite after his hunting party had left the forest.

A sharp sound suddenly cut through the slow music.

On cue, Aimee appeared behind the grave as Queen Myrtha.

Sensing the spirit queen, Hilarion stood up and looked around uneasily.

Fearing the wilis arrival, he fled the forest.

Myrtha danced into the glade, marking the start of her solo.

Gemma watched from the sidelines, following the steps she now knew so well in her head.

The evil queen beckoned towards the wings for the wilis to join her.

Gemma had to lead her line of the *corps* onto the stage.

She took a deep breath, and ran into the moonlit forest glade.

The audience was clapping madly and cheering. It was over. The opening night was done and dusted, and everything had been just perfect.

Gemma was elated. She had done everything right, and best of all, she had loved every minute of it.

The production went off without a hitch the rest of the week, and the next week. Every night people came from all over Johannesburg, Pretoria, and even some from Cape Town and Durban, packing out the theatre to see the production and be part of the SA Ballet Academy's centenary celebration.

It was Thursday afternoon. The final night's production was that night. Exams were over, school broke up for the

December holidays tomorrow, and life, Gemma thought, was just peachy.

She was sitting in the summerhouse with Marley and Dineo. The girls were discussing the past two weeks, the performances, the few oopses here and there that other dancers had had, and the glowing reviews in the newspaper about Dineo and Ethan's lead performances.

"Gemma?" One of the Grade 7 students popped his head into the summerhouse. "Ms Dubois wants to see you."

Concern wrinkled Gemma's brow. "About what?"

"Dunno. Something about Aimee feeling ill. Says she looks like she's seen a ghost."

"What?" Gemma looked from Marley to Dineo and back to Marley again. "Seen a ghost?"

"It's just an expression," Dineo said flatly.

Marley jumped up excitedly. "Or Emily!"

Gemma looked at Dineo who just shook her head and waved the other two girls out the summerhouse. "Go. I'll find you later."

The girls ran out of the summerhouse, down the stone stairs and towards Ms Dubois' classroom.

"I just can't do it, I'm sorry!" Aimee was saying to Ms Dubois as Gemma and Marley burst through the classroom door.

Naledi, Amber and a handful of other students had formed a ring around Aimee who was holding up one hand to her forehead and waving the other wildly in the air in great elaborate movements. "My nerves are shot."

"Ah, Gemma!" the teacher cried when she saw her. "You are here, good, good. Aimee says she cannot dance tonight. She is feeling too sick."

"I have to go rest," Aimee said, fluttering her eyelashes and fanning her face as Naledi and Amber escorted her out of the classroom.

"What happened?" Gemma asked.

"I was walking past the classroom and heard her scream," Zack gushed. "When I came in, she was staring out the window, eyes big as Cook Sheila's dinner plates and her face was hectically white. I swear, it looked like she had actually seen a ghost!"

"Well, we all know there's no such things as ghosts, so it must have been something else," Gemma said innocently.

Zack shrugged. "She looked weird, man."

"Oh Gemma, Gemma, Gemma!" Ms Dubois clasped Gemma's face between her hands. "Are you ready for tonight?"

Act 2 was about to begin. Gemma was waiting in the wings with Charles. She felt like she was going to get sick. She was shaking, her legs felt disconnected from her body, her heart was racing, and her tummy was a gurgle of nervous energy.

You can do this. You can do this.

The music started, and her heart leapt with fright. She knew she had to get her nerves under control.

Her eyes drifted over the stage where fake mist was rising from the forest glade. In the mist, she saw a face. Then a body. It was Emily. She was standing on the stage looking right at Gemma. She smiled at her, then raised her hand to her heart and extended it to Gemma.

Gemma understood.

Aimee *had* seen Emily that day, and the ghostly young dancer was making sure Gemma got her chance to dance.

This was Emily's gift to Gemma, to say thank you.

As the curtain began to rise, Emily's smiling form dissolved in the mist.

Gemma instantly felt different.

She remembered why she was here. To dance.

And tonight she wouldn't just dance for her own love of ballet, but for Emily's too.

"This is for you, Emily," she whispered.

Gemma closed her eyes.

She pushed her fears aside.

And allowed the music to carry her away.

The audience was on their feet, clapping and shouting bravo!

Dineo and Ethan stood at the front of the stage, with the other soloists behind them, and the *corps de ballet* in rows at the back.

The lead performers walked forwards and curtsied and bowed appreciatively to the audience.

Gemma couldn't believe she was there, upfront with the soloists. She couldn't help the huge grin that had spread across her face. As unballet-like as it was to stand there grinning, Gemma didn't care. She was on top of the world.

The excitement backstage and in the dressing room afterwards was off the charts. The dancers laughed and joked, still high on the adrenaline of being on stage, and filled with excitement for the after party that always followed a production's final night.

Gemma, Marley and Dineo had stripped off their costumes, hurriedly wiped off most of their makeup and pulled on some sweats before running out the dressing room to join the party.

They collided with the entire SS outside the door.

"Just because you got to do my dance for one night, doesn't mean you've cracked this school. You were still just the understudy," Aimee scoffed at Gemma.

Dineo clicked her tongue. "Oh plug it already, Atherton!" she said, pushing past the SS, and dragging Gemma and Marley with her.

Gemma and Marley doubled over with laughter as they ran. They'd never seen Dineo act so fierce before!

"I like this Neo!" Marley teased as she ran.

Teachers, parents and VIP guests milled around in the Great Ballroom sipping drinks and eating fancy snacks.

Tables with drinks and food had been set up on the landing outside the ballroom for the students, who were generally running amok in the school.

The girls grabbed something to eat, and plonked themselves down on the stone stairs overlooking the lawns.

"Hellooooo ladies!" Mitch said, appearing out of nowhere from behind them, and bounding down the stairs to where Marley was sitting.

"That was some pretty sick dancing tonight, Gemma James," Ethan said, jumping down onto the step that

Gemma was sitting on, and making himself comfortable next to her.

"I do not know what that means, but I do hope it means it was good?" a small, faint voice floated up from the garden below.

"Emily!" Gemma cried, jumping up.

"You did not think that we would leave without saying goodbye, did you?" Emily asked.

"Uh well …"

"Of course not! We spirits never leave unfinished business here on earth, as you well know." She smiled, a ghostly sparkle in her eye. "I am delighted you got the opportunity to dance a solo performance, Gemma. I do not think it did Aimee any harm to have a night off?"

"You didn't have anything to do with that, did you?"

"What, me? Not at all. I may have paid her a little visit," Emily shrugged, looking up at the stars innocently.

Gemma, Marley, Dineo, Mitch and Ethan all laughed out loud.

Emily smiled softly now at Gemma. "We are a lot alike, are we not? I know what you did for me tonight. I heard you, on the stage. And so this is for you," Emily turned and floated across the lawn. Oliver wafted out of the shadows, joining her. "We bid you farewell!" Emily called, as she and Oliver waved. "We will see you again!"

And with that the two ethereal figures danced a beautiful whirling, twirling *pas de deux* across the dewy grass into the night.

THE END

Hello, from Bronwyn!

Did you enjoy Gemma's story? It's the first book in the SA Ballet Academy series, with more stories about Gemma, Marley, Dineo, Ethan and Mitch to come!

Become part of the SA Ballet Academy Fanclub and get cool content about your favourite characters, sneak peeks at upcoming books and free stuff, all just for you! Sign up at www.saballetacademy.com/fanclub/

I love ballet (I did ballet until I was 17 years old), dance and magical worlds where you can lose yourself, meeting fantastical characters along the way. Which is why I enjoy writing urban fantasy books about ordinary girls just like you and me, but with a magical twist!

Book number 2 in the SA Ballet Academy series is coming out in 2017, with another three books planned for the next two years. And I promise you, there are plenty of wonderful characters and more than just a little magic in store for you!

When not lost in thought dreaming up new plotlines involving sassy Gemma, marvellous Marley, determined

Dineo, funnyman Mitch and dreamy Ethan, I run my own writing and editing business from my home in the beautiful Garden Route region of South Africa.

I love hearing from new SA Ballet Academy fans. You can get in touch with me on info@saballetacademy.com or www.saballetacadmy.com, or follow me (if you're 13+ and with your parents' permission, of course!) on my SA Ballet Academy pages on Facebook, Instagram and Pinterest.

You can also let me know what you thought about Dance with your Heart by posting your very own book review on Goodreads (Psst, ask an adult to help you if you're younger than 13!).

Thank you for your wonderful support! I can't wait to share the rest of Gemma's story and her amazing adventures with you.

Much love,
Bronwyn

Acknowledgements

Thanks to…

My boys Miles, Cayden, Cullum and Finn, for putting up with my furious (and often late-night) writing sessions.

My mom Carol and my dad Owen for paying for my ballet classes, which nurtured my love for ballet (and all those trips to the annual eisteddfods!)

My mom for watching the kids, which allowed me to finally get the book finished and published, and my dad for carting the kids around so I could have more time to write.

My sister Colleen for the many hours spent consulting on the book, typesetting the book and of course, conceptualising, illustrating and creating the gorgeous cover.

My friends Sabine Bittle, Pam Viljoen, Kat Silver, Taylor Williams, Tracey Brogan and Megan Clous for their invaluable feedback during the writing and editing process, and Donna Bartell and Kerry Jones for providing 'best friend' character inspiration.

My tutor Helen Brain who helped kickstart the journey six years ago that resulted in this book, and author Rachel Morgan for always providing such useful advice on writing and publishing as an independent author in South Africa.

Photographer Lauge Sorensen for organising the dancers and props for the cover shoot, and for the beautiful cover photos.

And to all the wonderful ballet people I have met who have provided inspiration for Gemma's story: my first ballet best friend, Deseré Linden; my ballet teacher Laurine Symons; and the teachers and dancers at the Johannesburg Youth Ballet (1993/4).

Made in the USA
San Bernardino, CA
24 November 2017